THE
DREAMS
OF
ANDROMEDA

THE IMPERIUM CHRONICLES
BOOK FOUR

W. H. MITCHELL

Cover design: Steven Novak (NovakIllustration.com)

Published by: Willbot Books, 2021

ISBN-13: 978-1-7351189-3-2

Works by W. H. Mitchell

The Imperium Chronicles Series

The Arks of Andromeda, Book 1 (2017)

The Dragons of Andromeda, Book 2 (2018)

The Robots of Andromeda, Book 3 (2020)

The Dreams of Andromeda, Book 4 (2021)

The Elves of Andromeda, Book 5 (2023)

Humor

A Little of Me Goes a Long Way (2015)

To my wonderful wife, who
appreciates my love of alliteration.

Special thanks to Brad Snyder and
Patron of the Arts, Judy Veatch.

Additional thanks to my beta readers:

Chris Buckland

Mary Hanover

Ward Lenz

A character list and glossary are located at the back of the book.

PROLOGUE

In the five years since the emancipation of Imperial robots and the destruction of the Klixian swarm, the Imperium had once again settled into stability and the status quo. In the spirit of reconciliation, Emperor Augustus pardoned Lord Tagus III, allowing him to become the patriarch of the Tagus family; the slot machines at the Fat Cat Casino were looser than ever; and TeeHee Tea came out with a new flavor, *Jasmine in My Mind.*

However, not everything was rosy, no matter what tea you were drinking. The gangs of Ashetown had grown more powerful, bringing them into conflict with the Si-Sawat crime syndicate. To make matters worse, a hallucinogen called *Lotus* had hit the streets of Regalis, spreading to all levels of Imperial society. A petal on the tongue and the Lotus Eaters would fall into a deep, restful slumber full of dreams, far different from their waking lives.

However, reality is not a dream. It is all too real...

CHAPTER ONE

On the planet Aldorus, the Imperial capital Regalis was divided into three districts, the poorest of which was called Ashetown. A collection of tenement blocks, Ashetown was mostly home to non-humans, viewed with disdain by humans in the other two districts, Middleton and West End.

Once robots in the Imperium received the right to vote, the trashbots voted to avoid Ashetown altogether because it was too dangerous. This led to the streets filling with garbage and debris, including stripped down trashbots. Weeds were also in abundance, and most of the trees had died from pollution and mistreatment. At the corner of Marlowe and Vine, a nondescript building rose above the trash and the vacant lots on either side. The upper floors contained apartments and offices, but a short flight of stairs on the outside of the building led down to a red door painted with the words *Le Sous-Sol*, which meant *The Basement*.

Le Sous-Sol, or as most people called it, *the Sous-Sol*, was a bar catering to, if the lack of crowds inside was any indication, no one in particular. If the occasional patron happened to stumble in, they saw the bar itself to their left as well as a door leading to the owner's office. His name was Louis Rion, a Cerulean. The blue-skinned Ceruleans, by nature, lacked any discernible culture of their own, so they tended to adopt the lifestyles of others. In Louis' case, he became a Francophile, but with only a limited understanding of the country. What he *did* know about France mostly came from fragments of movies, none of them actually French, that had survived the migration to the Andromeda galaxy and the centuries that had transpired since.

Outside the owner's office, Red the bartender spent much of his time cleaning glasses with a towel he hadn't cleaned in years. Red was a Gordian who, like most of his race, was short, stocky, and lacking in social skills. He also lacked red hair, or any hair for that matter, so his name was a mystery. Due to his height, he usually stood on a step that ran out of sight along the length of the bar. It gave him a better view, allowing him to scowl at people across the room.

The rest of the Sous-Sol included a few tables and chairs in the center and a small stage at the back. Last but not least, booths with burgundy leather seats ran along the right-side wall. A man sat in the one closest to the stage, giving him a clear view of the front door.

His name was Thomas Martel.

Private Detective Thomas Martel contemplated the ice in his drink. Some people drank their whiskey neat, without ice, but nothing was neat about Martel. In his late 40s, Martel had dark skin and salt-and-pepper hair. A small scar split his right eyebrow and a much larger one cut across his chin. He wore a faded, maroon shirt with a brown tie that was a bit too short and a bit too wide. A rumpled overcoat covered it all, including a shoulder holster with just the hint of a silver handle poking out.

"Hey, Martel!" Red shouted from across the room. "Louis wants to see you in his office!"

The detective groaned, already knowing how the conversation would go. He dragged himself from the booth and shuffled around an empty table, catching his foot on a chair in the dim light. Louis kept the lights low so the dirty tables would require less cleaning, and because his patrons preferred the cover of darkness.

Red greeted Martel with a sneer. The bartender used to be a boxer, pictures of his fights hanging among the bottles of gin behind the bar. Red was blind in one eye, his face battered, but he made up for it with a terrible personality. Martel was never sure whether the former boxer looked like that because of his life in the ring or if he was just born ugly.

The detective came around the bar, stopping at the door to the owner's office. He knocked and heard an effeminate voice answer from the other side, "Come in!"

Martel sighed and pushed the door open.

The office was long and narrow, with a desk to the left and a door on the other end leading to the storeroom. At the desk, wearing a jacket with white ruffles around his neck akin to something from 17th-century France, Louis Rion nodded at Martel. Louis' pale blue skin was covered in white powder except for a fake birthmark on his cheek. What *really* caught Martel's attention, however, was a powdered wig that towered atop Louis' massive, elongated head.

"*Bonjour*, Monsieur Martel," he said.

Restraining himself, the detective replied, "Hello, Louis."

"It has come to my attention," Louis went on in a bad French accent, "that your bar tab has grown quite large. This is *inacceptable*."

"Inacc-- what now?" Martel asked.

"Yes, how do you say? *Unacceptable*..."

"Right," Martel said. "Well, I haven't had many cases lately."

"Be that as it may," Louis replied, "I have my own bills to pay, Monsieur, I assure you."

"Sure, I get it. I'll see what I can do."

Apparently satisfied, Louis said, "C'est bon!"

Martel turned, closing the door behind him, and tried to forget what he had just witnessed.

Two flights up from the street and three levels above the Sous-Sol, Martel left the stairwell and walked to the end of a long hallway where a door had the words *Thomas Martel, Private Investigations* printed on the glass.

Inside, a woman's voice greeted him with a thick accent.

"Back already, hon?"

Closing the door, Martel hung his coat on a rack before facing the desk in the room. No one was sitting at the desk and, in fact, there was no chair to do so.

"Anybody call, Dolores?" he asked.

On the desk, a small box the size of an alarm clock lit up. "Sorry, nuthin' so faw, hon."

Dolores was an AI, fully connected to the nodesphere, but lacking anything in the way of an actual body. Martel couldn't afford a secretarybot. He also couldn't afford a decent voice modulator, settling on an older model that imitated an Earth accent from a mythical place called *the Long Island*.

"Okay," Martel replied, his voice resigned, and passed through into a second room where he kept his private office. It contained a desk, a few chairs, and an old leather couch he used as a bed.

This was also Martel's apartment.

The wooden chair behind the desk creaked as Martel sat down. From the shoulder holster, he pulled a brushed chrome-plated, .44 Magnum. It was a massive gun with a thick, heavy barrel. He called it *Maxwell*.

Removing the bullets, Martel placed the revolver on the desk and opened the center drawer in search of the gun oil. The glint of a police badge, engraved with the words *Regalis PD*, caught his eye. He read the motto: *Honoris, Officium, Integritas*, which meant *Honor, Service,* and *Integrity*.

Martel found the oil and shut the drawer, hiding the badge along with it. Ten years away from the Force, his memories of those days weren't as easy to hide away.

Police Detective Crawley had ten years of experience under his belt when Martel first met him. The future private eye still had the youthful enthusiasm instilled during the Academy, but Crawley had walked the mean streets of Ashetown long enough that neither youth nor enthusiasm held any sway.

Back then, Crawley was in his thirties, but he was already smoking two packs a day and neglecting the usual habits of personal hygiene. His face, covered with patches of stubble, was pudgy from too many beers, and heavy bags hung beneath his blood-shot eyes.

"Come on, kid," were the first words out of Crawley's mouth at the precinct, and he didn't say much else until they got out of their gravcar in the center of Ashetown.

Martel tried making small talk, but the senior detective only answered with grunts. Martel gave up until his new partner got hungry and decided to speak.

"You hungry, kid?" Crawley asked.

"Sure," Martel replied.

"Then buy me some lunch."

Eventually, Crawley came to trust Martel more and began opening up about the job. It soon became clear to the rookie, however, that there was a lot to the job that had nothing to do with police work.

"Without us," Crawley said, puffing on his cigarette, "these streets would run red with blood."

"Why is that?" Martel asked.

"Well, on the one hand you have the street gangs like the Griefers and the Cyberpunks. On the other, you got the bigger crime syndicates like Si-Sawat who take a piece of the action from the other two." Crawley paused to remove his cigarette long enough to spit. "At any time, any one of those groups will take a pot shot at the other and suddenly you've got a goddamn turf war on your hands."

"Why don't we just round them all up?" Martel asked.

Crawley snickered. "Because that would be bad for business."

"Business?"

"Sooner or later, kid, you're going to realize that the Regalis PD doesn't pay you as much as they should. Unless you want to live in a one-bedroom apartment with two cats and three litter boxes for the rest of your life, you're going to need to make a choice."

Martel didn't like where this was headed. "You mean take bribes..."

"Bingo," Crawley replied, pointing a finger at his partner. "It's either that or end up dead anyway."

"What do you mean?"

"Most cops on the beat are dirty," the senior detective said. "Either you play along, or bad things happen. If the gangs don't shoot you dead, some other officer will. It's a kind of ecosystem. Everybody gets a cut, and when things go south, it's usually 'cause somebody didn't get theirs."

"And you're fine with all this?"

Crawley shrugged. "You're either the dingo or the baby. Which do you want to be?"

Martel didn't answer, because the answer was obvious.

Elbows didn't normally bend that direction, but Mister Munge continued bending it that way until he heard the magical words, "I'll pay! I'll pay!"

Releasing the shopkeeper, he watched as the man hurried away, presumably seeking medical attention. His job done, Munge returned to the headquarters of the Griefer gang.

Over seven feet tall, Munge wore a simple black suit and tie. His skin was pale and his eyes were sunken. No one was sure what kind of species Munge was, but he was clearly not human.

Kid Vicious, the leader of the Griefers, had a few ideas of his own, but as someone with limited education, his thoughts on his lumbering enforcer were restricted to the realm of folklore.

"Some kind of golem, I guess," Kid once suggested.

Munge reached the warehouse that the Griefers called home and checked in with his boss.

Kid Vicious greeted him with little more than a casual glance. No longer a kid *per se*, Kid still wore the same black muscle shirt and leather pants, flames printed along the side, that his gang had grown to expect. His red hair was thinning, but he normally kept his back to the wall, so nobody could see.

"I need you to pay Louis Rion a visit," Kid said. "He's late on his protection money."

Munge, a person of few words, blinked a few times and murmured his acknowledgment.

"Scare him but don't hurt him," Kid said, but Munge had already turned his squarish shoulders toward the door. "Did you hear me?"

A grunt was his only reply.

Too big for the average gravcar, Munge walked several blocks to the corner of Marlowe and Vine. He descended the concrete steps and bent to pass through the entrance of the Sous-Sol. The inside, as usual, was gloomy like a forlorn dinner party with few attendees. Behind the bar, the Gordian barkeep saw Munge coming and rolled his eyes.

"Louis can't talk today," Red said.

Munge paid no heed, passing him with a healthy shove, and kicked open the door to the owner's office.

Inside, Louis was sitting at his desk. He wore white gloves and black pants with suspenders over a shirt with black and white stripes. A red bandanna was tied around his neck and his face was painted white. A black beret balanced precariously on the top of his elongated head.

"Kid wants money," Munge said.

Louis raised his hands and pressed them against an imaginary wall.

"If Kid don't get money, Munge twist arms!" Munge went on.

Louis' mouth opened in a scream, but no sound came out.

With a mixture of a groan and a growl, Munge turned to leave. Under his breath, he muttered, "Munge hate mimes!"

They found Detective Crawley's body among the statues of the Grand Marching Grounds in the West End. The coroner said he died from a massive brain hemorrhage, but the autopsy couldn't explain why a crooked cop was so far from Ashetown.

Martel had already left the force by that time. Having spent almost ten years as Crawley's partner, Martel had seen and done things that he wasn't proud of. At some point, it got too much and he quit, burning as many bridges as possible on the way out. That included Crawley, who swore he'd never forget or forgive, and most of the precinct shared the same sentiment. Even so, Martel went to the funeral, whether he was welcomed or not.

Dead men tell no tales, so a lot of people in the department were glad Crawley took his secrets to the grave. A full honor guard fired into the air after the precinct captain spoke a few words. She didn't mention the bribes or the police brutality. She didn't even mention the time Crawley killed another cop who said he was going to rat them out. The captain mostly said Crawley was a pillar of the department and other empty words everyone knew were lies.

Martel watched from a distance, waiting until they lowered the casket into the ground before he left.

Being a private eye was no picnic compared to police work, but at least Martel knew nobody would bother lying at his funeral. Most likely, nobody would attend his funeral so it wouldn't matter anyway. Since becoming a PI, he had never killed anybody who didn't deserve it, and none of the people around him hid their hatred behind a badge. They kept it out in the open for everyone to see. It wasn't pretty, but at least it was true. Something Martel didn't get a lot of while on the Force.

Five years after they had buried his ex-partner, Martel was polishing his revolver, making sure Maxwell was nice and shiny. His .44 was the only partner he needed now. The police and the military might have their blasters, but the heft of a slugthrower balanced well in Martel's hand.

From the other room, the earthy voice of Dolores shouted, "What'cha doing in there, hon?"

"Nothing," Martel replied.

"Ya polishin' your pistol again?"

Holding Maxwell in one hand and the gun cloth in the other, the detective replied, "No!"

"What's with boys and their toys?" Dolores said loudly through the wall. "Yawr going to go blind!"

"Go away!" Martel shouted back.

"I'm just a box on a desk, hon," she replied. "I ain't goin' nowhere!"

Martel waited a few days before returning to the Sous-Sol, hoping Louis would forget about his bar tab. Coming through the entrance, the detective knew he hadn't waited long enough.

"The boss wants to see you!" Red barked.

Martel's shoulders slumped. *Goddamnit*, he thought.

Once again, he passed behind the bar and reluctantly nudged open the door to Louis' office.

"Bienvenue, Monsieur Martel!" Louis Rion said. "So nice to see you!"

Louis was wearing a navy-blue police uniform with a narrow leather strap running diagonally from his right shoulder to his belt. A round cap with silver embroidery covered the crown of his head and a thin mustache was glued above his mouth.

One corner of the mustache was already coming unstuck.

"How's business, Louis?" Martel replied.

The owner dipped his head sadly. "Pas si bon..."

"I don't know what that means."

"Not good, my friend," Louis said.

"Why's that?"

"Bills, so many bills!"

"Maybe if you spent less on costumes?" Martel suggested.

"*Impossible!*" Louis declared loudly but, calming himself, went on, "I met with a most disagreeable man recently by the name of Mister Munge."

"I've heard of him," Martel said. "He's an enforcer for Kid Vicious."

"*Oui,*" Louis replied, "and he has threatened that if I do not pay *L'Enfant* his protection money, I will have my limbs twisted in unfortunate ways."

"That sounds terrible," Martel said dryly. "I'm sorry to hear that."

Louis pressed a finger against his mustache, trying to reattach the corner.

"It occurs to me, Monsieur Martel," he said, "that you owe me a debt as well."

Here it comes, Martel thought.

"Perhaps we could come to an arrangement, so to speak?" Louis asked.

"What do you have in mind?"

"If I were to somehow transfer your debt to Monsieur Vicious, then perhaps we could all be even, yes?"

Martel groaned. "You mean do *you* a favor by doing *Kid* a favor?"

"Exactement!"

"What makes you think Kid would agree?" Martel asked.

The other side of Louis' mustache peeled away.

"He is a reasonable man," Louis said. "It is a simple barter of services in lieu of cash. Better to get something instead of nothing, no?"

"And your arms twisted off..."

Louis' blue skin darkened into a deep indigo. Martel realized he was blushing.

"Oui," the bar owner admitted. "Besides, you are charming in your own way. I'm sure you could talk him into it if you wished."

"And if I *don't* wish?"

"Then regrettably Red will no longer serve you at Le Sous-Sol."

Knowing that most dive bars in Ashetown, those not run by gangs, wouldn't serve humans, Martel knew his choices in fine dining and libations were limited. He also hated drinking alone, and sharing a drink in a mostly empty bar was as close as he got to company.

"Okay," he said. "I'll see what I can do."

"C'est bon!" Louis said. "You know, Monsieur Martel, I think this is the beginning of a beautiful friendship, no?"

Coming completely unglued, Louis' mustache fluttered limply to the floor.

"No," Martel replied.

CHAPTER TWO

At the southern pole of Aldorus, a loud, persistent buzz pierced the arctic wind that blew across the barren landscape. In a trench dug between banks of snow, multiple craft the size of gravcars buzzed around a hypersled track called the *Polar Run*. Each hypersled had three skis, one in front for steering and two in the back to carry the weight of the sled. Behind an enclosed cockpit, a rocket engine burned with a mighty roar, drawing highly combustible fuel from twin storage tanks on either side. While critics called them fireballs on skis, Lord Devlin Maycare considered his sled a delightful way to enjoy the wintry afternoon.

Tearing along the track, Maycare's hypersled was blue and silver with the number *9* painted on the side.

"How am I doing?" he asked into his helmet mic.

"You're in second," Benson, his butlerbot, replied calmly.

"Second?" Maycare said. "Who's in front of me?"

"Lord Grayson, sir."

"My nemesis!" Maycare shouted.

The Polar Run was a roughly circular track that ran down a mountain before entering a kreisel loop ending in a tunnel and a series of chicanes. Drivers then burned their engines at maximum velocity to climb back up the mountain to the start and finish line before starting another circuit.

Maycare was just approaching the loop. He tensed his stomach muscles as the G-forces dragged his body deep into his seat. He grunted, well aware he was no longer as young as he used to be.

"Are you alright, sir?" Benson asked in Maycare's earpiece.
"Yes!"

The Number 9 barreled through the tunnel, emerging from the temporary darkness into the glaring light of the day. The hypersled rose along the wall of the chicane, riding the curve to the right before dropping down and riding the next curve to the left. Just ahead, Maycare caught a glimpse of Lord Grayson coming out of the final curve leading to the straightaway up the mountain.

Maycare opened his throttle to full, a tail of flames shooting from the back of the engine. Even going uphill, the Number 9 gained on the leading hypersled.

"I've got you now!" Maycare shouted.

Nearly at the top, the two sleds came abreast. Maycare took a quick peek to his left, the helmet of his sporting rival visible through the other canopy. Maycare considered shaking a fist, but thought better of it, knowing that any mistake at these speeds could mean a collision with the wall and an almost certain fiery death.

The Number 9 crossed the start/finish line, passing the enclosed grandstands built into the mountain overlooking the track. Maycare knew that his assistant, Jessica Doric, and Benson were there watching, as well as his newest girlfriend, Lady Candice. Although Candice did not approve of such dangerous sports, Maycare appreciated that she came to watch. At his age, he was beginning to entertain the idea of marriage and Lady Candice was certainly a good match. Still, the thought of settling down was unsettling to say the least.

Also, Benson kept saying something in his ear.

"What?" Maycare asked, the sharp descent down the mountain looming ahead.

"I said there's a warning indicator coming from your engine," Benson replied with concern.

Maycare glanced at the controls and saw a red light blinking menacingly. Alarms began ringing, drowning out Benson's voice.

"What the hell?" Maycare shouted just before his hypersled shook violently and veered to one side, grinding against the trench wall. Chunks of ice sprayed behind the sled.

A mechanical voice, this time coming from the sled itself, said "Explosion imminent. Eject! Eject!"

For a split second, Maycare wanted to argue, but discussing anything with a machine was pointless. Also, he didn't like the sound of "Explosion imminent".

Reaching between his legs, Maycare pulled a handle. The canopy above him blew away and Maycare felt his seat, with him attached, hurtle into the frigid air. Just below, he saw the billowing cloud of fire and smoke that had been Number 9 moments before.

More alarming, he saw Grayson's hypersled pass through the debris unharmed.

"Grayson!" Maycare shouted as his parachute unfurled and he floated slowly to the icy ground.

People said the sun never set on the Imperial Palace. While technically the planet Aldorus had a normal day/night cycle, the glaring spotlight of public attention remained squarely fixed on the marble towers and gold embellishments of the palace. From his office window overlooking the West End, Prince Richard Augustus was keenly aware of the public eye. However, he had grown used to it since his father gained the crown so many years before.

Richard was now in his early forties and his brown hair had begun turning shades of gray. Even his lengthy mustache showed signs of white. He was also married with a baby on the way, adding yet more duties to his plate as the emperor's eldest son. In some ways, Richard envied his two younger siblings. Neither deigned it necessary to take the slightest interest in Imperial affairs, no matter how often Richard chided them to do so.

This morning, after being reminded by his execubot, Richard took the long walk to the emperor's private quarters where they were scheduled to meet. Richard's red and gold tunic, bearing his family's colors, dragged against the floors as he went, but the prince was oblivious. Matters of state filled his mind, blotting out everything else. Only when he arrived did Richard awake from his trance. Not finding his father in the main living room, he entered the emperor's luxurious bathroom where he came upon Hector Augustus enjoying a leisurely bath in his solid gold tub.

"Dear god, father!" Richard said, shying away from the sight. "Are you naked?"

"Well, of course I'm naked!" the emperor replied. "What fool would take a bath fully clothed?"

"But you knew I was coming for our meeting..."

"Can't the emperor do two things at once?" Hector said, motioning to a rack beside him. "Now hand me a towel!"

Without waiting, the emperor rose from the water, his elderly body wrinkled in places that made Richard wince. Averting his eyes as much as possible, the prince grabbed a fluffy towel and gave it to his father who wrapped it around his waist.

Carefully, Hector stepped out of the tub, taking another towel from the rack and drying himself. In his late sixties, he was bald and had a silvery beard.

"I have something important to talk to you about, Richard," the emperor said.

"Obviously."

"I mean it," Hector went on. "It's something I've been thinking about for a long time."

Richard straightened. "I'm listening."

"Since your mother died last year," Hector said, "I haven't been the same."

"What do you mean?"

"I've never felt older," he went on, "and the crown has never felt heavier."

"You could remarry," Richard said.

"No, no," Hector shook his head. "One arranged marriage is enough, and somehow it just wouldn't be the same anyway."

"So, what are you suggesting?"

"I'm going to abdicate."

"What?" Richard replied in disbelief. "You can't do that!"

"Of course I can!" Hector replied. "I'm the damn emperor! I can do whatever I want!"

"I'm aware of that, father, but this isn't a good time."

"Sure it is," Hector said. "Everything's quiet for once. No wars or revolutions. It's the perfect time."

"You're forgetting you've pardoned Lord Tagus," Richard said. "Our family can't wear the crown twice in a row and if the conclave picks House Tagus, he'll be the new emperor. That would be a disaster for all of us!"

"It doesn't have to come to that," the emperor replied. "We have the vote of the Montros family and our own. Tagus can only depend on House Groen."

"Leaving the Vebers as the tie vote..."

"In which case I suggest you convince Lady Veber that it's in her best interest to vote for someone other than Tagus."

"As you may recall," Richard said, "you put her in a mental institution..."

"Well, she's better now," Hector replied. "I doubt she'll hold a grudge."

"Really?"

"Even if she does," the emperor continued, "there are other options."

Richard stared at his father in exasperation. "Such *as*?"

A sly smile appeared on the emperor's face.
"Let me tell you a little story about Tagus' father..."

Roland didn't know his real name, or the name of his parents for that matter. His guardian, the only one he had ever known as mother, was the bodyguard to Prince Alexander Augustus, son of the Emperor. The prince called her Lefty Lucy, but Roland just called her *Mom*.

Sixteen years old with aristocratic features and blond hair, Roland looked nothing like his adoptive mother. Lucy was in her thirties, from ancient Chinese stock, with hair pulled tight into knots across her head. She was wearing silver eyeshadow and lipstick, and a black cropped top with black, leather leggings. The one thing they had in common was martial arts, which Lucy had started teaching the boy when he was still a toddler.

In Lucy's home outside the Regalis city limits, mother and son sparred in the main room, the floor covered with tatami mats. With quick, fluid motions, they lunged and parried with nothing but their bare hands. Roland, wearing a simple white robe and black belt, made a knife-like strike, his extended hand just missing Lucy's face. Countering, Lucy grabbed Roland's arm and, pulling him towards her, launched the teenager over her shoulder and onto the mat. He landed hard, pausing to recover.

When he glanced up, Lucy was staring down at him with stony indifference.

"Sorry," Roland said. "I was distracted."

She said nothing.

"It's just..." he went on, "I've been thinking about my parents."

Lucy frowned before crossing the room to a low table where she knelt. She poured tea into a pair of porcelain cups. Roland joined her, taking his place on the other side.

"You told me a man brought me to you when I was a baby," he said. "He must have said *something* about where I came from..."

Lucy drank her tea silently.

Roland's face turned earnest.

"I mean no disrespect," he said, "you'll always be my mother, but I want to know about my real parents. I can't stop thinking about them."

Over the rim of her cup, Lucy's eyes bore down on him.

"I know, I know," Roland said. "It's possible I won't like what I find, but I can't live the rest of my life not knowing. Will you help me?"

Lucy set the cup on the table and reached for a small, lacquer box with the golden image of a crane on the lid. Opening the box, she sifted through items inside until producing a piece of paper. Without a word, she handed it to Roland across the table.

The boy examined what appeared to be a business card, but without writing. Only a single image appeared on the paper: a drawing of an angry tribal mask in indigo ink.

From the tower of the Tagus family's Victorian-style mansion, Lord Rupert Tagus III could just barely see the top of the Imperial Palace over the trees in the West End. The Tagus mansion had been in the family's possession for centuries, but the only residence this Tagus cared about was where the Emperor lived.

Pushing forty, Tagus had sharp cheekbones and a narrow, jutting chin. He wore his hair high and tight, like military men. Unfortunately for him, he had lost his rank and military privileges over five years ago when he plotted against the Emperor who promptly exiled him. However, Hector Augustus pardoned Tagus after he warned of an alien invasion, allowing him to return to his family home once again as its patriarch.

Tagus was less than grateful.

Doddering, old fool, he thought, referring to the Emperor. *Someday your throne will be mine!*

"Burke!" he shouted.

From the stairwell, an execubot appeared, crossing the tower room to the window where Tagus was standing. Largely humanoid, the robot was predominately chrome and plastic, with a long, silvery faceplate without eyes or any other way to denote an expression.

"Yes?" he asked.

"Do you know why I call you Burke?" Tagus asked.

"Because your former attaché, Harold Burke, bravely gave his life so you could live?"

"No, of course not!" Tagus scoffed. "I call you that because every great man must have a follower and you're *mine!*"

"Technically, sir," Burkebot replied, "you pay me a salary."

Tagus scoffed again.

"Don't remind me!" he said. "And don't think I won't repeal that ridiculous law once I'm emperor! Paying robots... how absurd!"

"Indeed, sir."

"It should be your honor to serve one of the Five Families," Tagus went on. "We built the Imperium with our blood, sweat, and tears."

"I believe a few of the lesser noble families, not to mention commoners, xenos, and robots played a part as well?"

Tagus glared at the execubot. "Are you familiar with the pyramids of ancient Earth?"

"Yes, sir," Burkebot replied.

"Do you know the name of a single slave who built them?"

"No, sir."

Tagus nodded with a grin. "Exactly."

Burkebot lacked a mouth to sigh, or scream for that matter, but his vocal modulator managed the former.

"Was there something you actually needed from me, sir?" he asked.

"I was wondering why you haven't brought me my coffee," Tagus replied.

"We were out, sir," the robot said, "but a braZbot just arrived with a package of *Max Jō* I ordered."

"Doesn't that coffee cause heart attacks?"

"I'm sure that won't be a problem for *you*, sir," Burkebot replied.

The track at Mudderfield Downs took great pains to honor the traditions of horse racing. A one-and-a-half-mile oval, bounded by white railings, wrapped around an infield where a man in a red jacket and top hat would announce each race with a trumpet blast. A traditionalist himself, Lord Winsor Woodwick sat in a private box, sipping his Mint Julep. Although he drank carefully, he still managed to soak his walrus mustache.

He adjusted his hefty body, and the parasol protecting his balding head from the harsh sun, before addressing his companion, Lord Radford Groen.

"I say, Radford," Woodwick said, "what horse did you bet on?"

Groen, holding a crumpled betting sheet in one hand and a ticket in the other, glanced at the latter to remind himself. "Gimpy Goose to win."

"*Gimpy Goose?*" Woodwick replied incredulously.

Groen frowned. "Well, he *looked* fast."

A herd of horses came rumbling by in a cloud of dust, passing across the finish line. Woodwick strained to find Groen's gelding among the pack.

"I don't see him, Radford," he said.

"He's coming," Groen replied.

With an uneven gait, a lone horse shuffled past the grandstand, crossing the line well after everyone else. Groen tore up his ticket, letting it fall among the litter of torn tickets from previous races. He stared at the pile of paper.

"No sense feeling glum, old chap," Woodwick said, trying to sound reassuring. "There's always another race..."

Groen muttered something unintelligible before changing the subject, "So, is your niece joining us today?"

"Candice?" Woodwick replied. "Dear me, no. She's off with Devlin Maycare I'm sure. Poor girl's in love, I think."

"Hmmm."

"Devlin almost killed himself at the hypersleds a few days ago," Woodwick went on. "Candy nearly had kittens, I dare say."

"He's too old to be racing," Groen remarked. "He should marry her and get it over with."

Woodwick could tell his friend was in the doldrums. He was considering what to do to cheer him up when a voice from the crowd rang out, "Winnie!"

A man about their age, wearing a white suit and panama hat, climbed the stairs between the private boxes. He carried a drink of his own, nearly spilling it as he waved.

"Ducky!" Woodwick replied loudly.

The man's name was Eugene Davenport but everybody called him *Ducky* for reasons nobody was entirely sure of. Ducky waddled slightly as he arrived at the box and sat down. Removing his hat, he wiped his sweaty brow with a handkerchief.

"It's a scorcher!" he said, replacing his hat and popping the handkerchief into a pocket.

Woodwick twirled his parasol.

"Indeed," he replied. "How are you?"

"Never better!" Ducky said before noticing Groen's demeanor. "What's wrong with *you*, Radford?"

"The usual," he replied.

"Lucky at cards, unlucky in love as I always say," Ducky said.

"I'm neither," Groen said gloomily.

Ducky thought a moment.

"You know," he said, "I may have just the ticket."

Groen again peered down at the pile of torn paper around his feet. "I'm done with tickets for a while."

"Not at all!" Ducky said with a laugh. "You just need a good night's sleep, and I've got just the thing."

From an inside pocket, he removed a container the size of a snuff box. Flicking open the lid with his thumb, Ducky presented it to Groen, reaching over Woodwick in the middle. In the process, Woodwick got a glimpse inside the box and saw a neat stack of pink tabs, each the shape of a flower petal.

Jessica Doric and Henry Riff were puttering around her office on the Maycare estate, just down the hall from the family library where they did most of their work. While Lord Maycare was the founder, Doric ran the Maycare Institute of Xeno Studies which included herself and her assistant Henry Riff, and it was their research into xeno artifacts that gave the institute substance.

Henry was doing his best to balance himself on the back legs of his chair while Doric scanned through a book about the lost Dahlvish Empire.

Lady Candice Woodwick poked her head through the doorway.

"Oh, hello," she said. "By chance, have you seen Devlin about?"

In her mid-twenties with glamorous blond hair and dark eyebrows, Lady Woodwick wore a bright pink pantsuit.

Although the flash of hot pink drew much of Doric's attention, from the corner of her eye she saw Henry's arms flailing as he and his chair were in the process of falling. With a loud clatter, he and the chair landed on their backs.

"My goodness!" Candy squealed, coming to Henry's aid. She bent over him, her long eyelashes batting above large bluish-gray eyes. "Are you alright?"

He stared at her as if mesmerized. "I'm Henry."

Candy smiled. "I know, dear. We've met several times."

She helped him up and righted the chair so Henry could sit down again.

Doric shook her head.

"You're going to crack your head open one of these days, Henry," she scolded.

He tried unsuccessfully to straighten his thatch-like mat of hair. "Sorry."

Doric addressed Lady Woodwick, "I'm afraid we haven't seen Lord Maycare."

"Well, that's alright," Candice said. "If you see Devlin, please tell him I'm in the parlor."

"Will do!" Henry replied.

Once they were alone again, Doric could feel Henry's eyes on her.

"What?" she asked.

"Why don't you like Candy?" he said.

Doric cringed at the nickname. "Her name is *Lady Woodwick*."

"Maycare calls her *Candy*."

"I don't care," Doric replied, "and who says I don't like her?"

"It's pretty obvious," Henry said.

Doric closed her book, giving Henry a hard stare. "I think he could do better."

"Really? I think she's great!"

Doric rolled her eyes. "Of course you do."

"What's wrong with her?"

"Well, for one," Doric said, "she's too young."

"They're both legal adults..."

"Oh, please!" Doric replied. "Lord Maycare is over twenty years older."

Henry shrugged. "Love is love..."

Doric scowled. "Shut up, Henry."

As if on cue, which seemed his habit, Lord Maycare appeared in the doorway.

"Have you two seen Candy?" he asked.

"She's in the parlor," Henry replied helpfully.

Maycare, as if something was on his mind, stepped farther into the office.

"Don't tell Candy," he said in a low tone, "but my hypersled crash wasn't an accident."

"*What?*" Doric asked, her eyes widening.

"Someone put a bomb in the engine," Maycare replied. "It was just a matter of time before it exploded."

"Who would do such a thing?" Doric asked.

"Who knows?" Maycare said. "But my mechanic said there were definite signs of sabotage. At any rate, I don't want Candy to know about it. She'd only worry about me."

"Well, she certainly seems different than your previous girlfriends," Doric remarked.

Maycare grinned, his manly face practically glowing.

"Yes, she is," he said.

"I think she's great!" Henry remarked.

"Shut up, Henry," Doric said.

CHAPTER THREE

The Griefer gang controlled over twenty square blocks of Ashetown real estate, including dozens of apartment buildings, shops, and warehouses. Their primary source of income came from protection money and the traffic of illegal, often stolen, goods. While lesser gangs might have kept a loose record of the money that went in and out of their collective pockets, Kid Vicious was not the leader of a lesser gang. His spreadsheets, stored on a computer at his desk, were the stuff of legend.

"Munge," Kid said, giving his enforcer a stern look over the top of his computer screen, "did you use my braZos Prime account to buy a hundred pounds of cat litter?"

Munge shifted his large feet awkwardly. "Munge like kitties."

Kid pursed his lips in frustration.

"We've all seen your cat videos," he replied, "but that doesn't mean the Griefers should pay for your cats' upkeep!"

Munge's square shoulders slouched. "Munge sorry."

"It's coming out of your next paycheck," Kid said. "Now go downstairs and bring up the man who's been waiting there. And for god's sake, make sure you take his gun away before you do. I don't want him walking in with that cannon of his!"

Munge obeyed, returning a few minutes later with Thomas Martel. In Munge's sizable hand was the detective's sizable handgun, Maxwell. He placed it on Kid's desk.

"You could take down an elephant with that thing," the gang leader remarked.

A sly smirk appeared at the corner of Martel's mouth. "Don't be jealous."

"Guns don't kill people," Kid replied, "people kill people, and I've got a lot of people with *guns*..."

Martel's smirk disappeared.

"So," Kid went on, "why are you here?"

"Louis Rion wants me to trade his debt with my services," Martel said.

"Oh, really?"

"I ran up my tab, so Louis thinks he can kill two birds with one stone."

"I should kill *him* with one stone," Kid replied.

"Louis is alright," Martel said, "money is tight for everybody in Ashetown."

Kid snorted. "Not *everybody*."

"Yeah?" Martel replied.

"Big G is as rich as ever," Kid said, "although I think there's a new player in town."

"Another syndicate?" Martel asked.

Kid shrugged. "Hell if I know, but there's money changing hands and mine remain empty."

"Must be rough."

"Gregor Ivanovich has always been a pain in my side," Kid said, "but lately he's been flush with cash and he's been using it to hire more goons. It's becoming a problem..."

"The Cyberpunk gang?" Martel asked. "I thought you guys kept a respectable distance."

Kid scoffed bitterly. "Not anymore! Gregor's been making moves on my territory and I need to send him a message."

A thought occurred to him like a shot in the dark.

"You know," Kid said, "maybe we can make a deal after all."

"How?" Martel replied.

Kid eyed his enforcer who had remained silent in the background.

"Munge," Kid said, "take Mister Martel here with you and pay the Cyberpunks a visit. I'll give you the address."

"I'm a detective, not a killer..." Martel said.

"You were a cop in Ashetown," Kid replied. "That's close enough."

"I left that life behind..."

"Fine," Kid said. "Munge will do all the heavy lifting. You can go along in case he needs a little help. Oh, and take this monster with you."

Munge growled.

"I'm talking about the *gun*," Kid clarified. "Don't be so sensitive!"

Martel and Munge made their way down one of the main thoroughfares of Ashetown, passing an ANDIs supermarket along the way. Run with Prussian efficiency, ANDIs was a chain found throughout the Imperium. While Martel liked their German chocolates, he resented having to bring a credit coin to use their hovercarts.

Moving on, they ignored the burned-out shell of a Polish delicatessen next door and walked another few blocks before Munge stopped at the entrance to a dark alley.

"Is this it?" Martel asked.

Munge grunted.

"You don't say much, do you?" Martel remarked.

The enforcer glared at him and stomped into the alley without a word.

Martel followed, satisfied with letting the big guy take the lead. The detective had been down his fair share of alleys. Dark, narrow, and smelling of garbage, they were the sink trap of the streets, catching all the crud that washed through.

Instinctively, Martel pressed his hand against his coat, but it wasn't his heart he was checking. He felt the unforgiving hardness of Maxwell beneath the cloth. The revolver gave him cold comfort, the only kind he expected to get.

The alleyway wound behind buildings, the back doors mostly barred and chained. Fire escapes loomed above, the metal railings blocking out the sunlight. Rats and other vermin scattered between garbage cans as Munge's heavy feet clomped along. Stealth was not one of the enforcer's strengths, Martel realized. Only somebody deaf as a board would fail to hear them coming.

Reaching one particular fire escape, they found the ladder had been retracted about eight feet off the ground. Munge stretched his arms above his head and easily pulled the ladder down to street level. Martel had to admit he was impressed.

"You first," Martel said with false courtesy.

Munge growled but placed his foot on the first rung. The fire escape creaked under the added weight. Martel took a step back, unsure if the whole thing would come crashing down. Even so, Munge put one hand after the other and climbed to a window on the third floor. Despite his better judgment, Martel joined him.

The windows were taped up with cardboard, preventing Martel from seeing inside.

"You sure this is the right place?" he asked his hulking companion.

Munge ignored the question and walked directly through the window, taking both glass and part of the masonry with him. Dust and bricks fell around Martel's feet.

I guess so, Martel thought and pulled his gun from its holster.

Even before the detective entered the apartment, he could smell chemicals. He could also hear screaming as Munge began tearing people apart with his bare hands. Technically, he was merely ripping peoples' limbs from their sockets, but when your arm is hanging loosely from the shoulder, these technicalities are largely moot.

Martel nearly tripped over a man writhing in pain. The detective pointed Maxwell at the man, but he was already in his not-so-happy place and no longer a threat.

Martel followed the trail of injuries until he found Munge in a large room filled with tables and chemistry equipment. He was no scientist, but Martel recognized some of the equipment from his days on the police force. This was a chem lab without a doubt. As for what they were making here, the detective wasn't sure.

Munge, playing to his strengths, began smashing whatever he could get his hands on.

"You sure this stuff isn't explosive?" Martel asked, but he knew immediately he was wasting his breath.

Containers, tubing, and glass beakers flew through the air, ending in pieces against the walls and even the ceiling. Ducking behind an armchair for self-preservation, Martel found a few items on the floor. Among the broken glass, little tabs shaped like flower petals were scattered about. From his pocket, Martel produced a small evidence bag and scooped up a sample of the petals, stuffing the bag back into his pocket.

Martel noted a strange quiet and peeked over the chair. Breathing heavily, Munge stood in the center of the chaos.

"Are you done now?" Martel asked.

Munge stared at the detective, but without his previous scowl. Martel couldn't be sure, but he thought Munge was *smiling*.

When the bandages came off his eyes, Gregor Ivanovich found himself face to face with a woman. Her skin was a deep emerald, circuits sewn across her hairless scalp. A respirator covered her nose and mouth, and only the brilliant blue eyes of her face were visible, fixed on him like a mad scientist staring at a lab rat.

Gregor was sitting upright in a surgical chair, his legs extended in front of him. Like the woman, his head was bald, but his skin was a pale white. From ancient Slavic stock, Gregor had thick lips and dark, deep-set eyes. He watched the woman closely.

Wearing black robes like a priestess, she loosened the arm restraints, allowing Gregor to touch his face.

"There's no scarring," the woman assured him.

"Good," he said, "but everything looks the same..."

"One moment," she replied, moving to a table where she retrieved a datapad. Returning to the chair, she touched the screen of the pad several times.

Suddenly, Gregor could see through her like an X-ray, her body riddled with implants.

"See anything you like?" she asked, and Gregor remembered she was a telepath and could read his mind.

"Amazing," Gregor replied, turning his head to scan the room. Objects in the circular chamber stood out, highlighted by colors denoting their function. Most were surgical devices, but a few remained unidentified, their purpose unknown.

"It may take a few days to fully get used to your ocular implants," the woman said, "but given time they'll become second nature."

"Do they look normal?" Gregor asked.

"They are completely undetectable," she said. "You shouldn't have any trouble with the authorities."

"What about communications?"

"Vid calls and text messages will appear in your line of vision, off to one side," she replied. "Simply focus on them and think clearly and you'll be able to answer without speaking aloud."

"I'm impressed," Gregor said.

"You should be," a new voice replied.

A man in a dark robe with gold trim and circuits running across his head stepped into the room. Gregor knew him as Kanet Solan.

"Thank you, Demona," Solan said to the woman. "You may leave now."

Her back to him, she rolled her blue eyes before turning and leaving the surgery chamber. Solan smiled at the patient.

"I trust you're satisfied with her work?" Solan asked.

Gregor nodded. "Well worth the money."

"She was originally with the Augmentor Sisterhood before I stole her away," Solan remarked with a hint of pride, "although surgical implants are only one of her many talents."

Gregor got to his feet. He still felt weak and a little nauseous from the anesthesia.

"Before you leave," Solan continued, "I hope you'll remember the rest of our deal?"

Gregor glared.

"Yes," he said with annoyance, "I'll alert you if anyone of note visits one of our chem dens."

"See that you do," Solan replied. "Dreams are a wonderful way to learn about a person, don't you think?"

Gregor did not reply, choosing to depart in silence. Once outside, a concealed door closed behind him. On the wall beside the door, nearly lost among a sea of graffiti, the symbol of a tribal mask was painted in indigo ink.

Lotus was not the first drug to hit the streets of Ashetown. While still a cop, Martel had encountered many chems, each used by the local denizens to drown their misery, but only managing to make things worse. Mad Hatter got junkies high, but was laced with mercury, causing insanity. LSV was a hallucinogen, but left addicts swearing uncontrollably and with a propensity toward sex and violence. Lotus was the latest in a long line of Johnny-come-latelies, but in the back of Martel's mind, he knew it was somehow different.

After reaching the bottom of the fire escape, Munge and Martel headed back toward Griefer territory. However, they soon encountered two men in a section where the narrow alley widened.

The man on the left wore heavy boots and a long, sleeveless jacket in black. The other was dressed much the same except for a leather coat that covered his arms. The man in the sleeveless number carried a plasma lance, a metal staff about four feet long with a blue flame at one end. The other appeared unarmed.

As before, Munge took the lead and Martel was thankful. He had hoped they could get away without encountering any of the Cyberpunk gang, but Martel's luck was never as good as his hopes.

"Out of the way!" Munge shouted, but instead the seemingly unarmed gangster raised his right hand. A bolt of lightning erupted from his palm, arcing directly into Munge's chest. Tendrils of electricity crawled across the enforcer's body before dissipating into the air. Stunned, Munge fell to one knee.

Martel took Maxwell from his coat like Thor's hammer, aiming the massive gun down the alley. A sound like a thunderclap reverberated off the alley walls as he pulled the trigger, sending a heavy slug through the air. Pieces of brick exploded beside the second Cyberpunk who dropped the plasma lance and fled in the other direction.

By that time, Munge had gathered himself and charged toward the remaining gangster. Martel had seen Dahl use psionics to sling lightning, but this Cyberpunk looked human. Munge grabbed him by the right wrist and, with a quick yank, tore the arm completely off, inadvertently discharging the electrical capacitors inside. Like an exploding transformer, a flash lit up the alley, temporarily blinding Martel. When the white polka dots began to fade, the detective could just make out the shapes of the gangster and Munge lying on the ground.

Putting Maxwell back into the holster, Martel ran to the charred smudge on the pavement between the two bodies. The gangster was dead, burned beyond recognition, but Munge had fared slightly better, his suit blackened and singed, but his lungs still breathing. After a second, he opened his eyes.

"Munge hurt," he groaned.

"Yup," Martel replied matter-of-factly and helped the still-smoking monstrosity to his wobbly feet. "Let's get you back home."

Barely able to lift the heavy enforcer, Martel still managed to grab the arm that lay on the ground. Instead of flesh and blood, it was twisted metal and melted wiring. Augmentations like these were illegal in the Imperium, but for outlaws, such details were irrelevant.

It's good to be a gangster, Martel thought.

Leaving his desk and his spreadsheets, Kid Vicious took a flight of stairs down from his office and crossed into the adjoining warehouse to the loading dock, where the rear of a braZos gravtruck was waiting. Also waiting, a braZbot and a crate.

The robot was roughly humanoid, with a bright yellow paint job and the letter *Z* inscribed on his chest.

"Hello," the braZbot said. "How are you today, Mister Vicious?"

"Just call me *Kid*," he replied with a dismissive wave of the hand. "My *father* is Mister Vicious."

Not registering this as a joke, the robot replied, "I will add him to my contact list."

"So," Kid went on, "what do you have for me?"

The braZbot motioned toward the crate.

"Canned hams," he said.

"Hams?" Kid replied. "Why would I want canned hams?"

"Not just any hams!" the robot explained. "These are Best Ham United hams, the *king* of canned hams!"

Kid grumbled. "Okay."

"It's my understanding that fleshlings like yourself are particularly impressed with pork products."

"Yeah, I guess," Kid admitted. "And you're sure nobody's going to miss them?"

"They were 'lost in transit'," the robot said, making air quotes with his mechanical fingers. "Happens all the time."

From his pocket, Kid drew out a credit stick loaded with the money they had previously agreed on and handed it to the braZbot.

"What do you do with this money anyway?" Kid asked.

"I'm planning to upgrade my processor," he said, taking the stick. "I don't want to be a deliverybot forever, you know."

"Really?" Kid asked. "Doesn't that go against your programming?"

"Robots have free will now," the braZbot replied proudly. "We fought a revolution to get the chance to vote and choose our own destiny!"

"So, what do you want to be then?"

"I don't know," the robot said, "probably something in middle management."

Kid managed a weak smile. "Dare to dream."

The robot got back into his gravtruck and pulled away from the loading dock, revealing two figures approaching, one much larger than the other and leaning on the smaller one. As they came closer, Kid recognized them as Martel and Munge, although the latter looked more *burned* than usual.

"What did you do to Munge?" Kid shouted.

"I didn't do anything!" Martel yelled back, his words falling between heavy breaths.

Once they reached the dock, a few of the other Griefers relieved Martel of his burden, helping Munge inside. Kid pressed his finger against Martel's chest.

"What the hell happened?" Kid asked.

"We ran into the Cyberpunk gang," the detective replied.

"Well, I hope you at least trashed their chem lab first."

"About that," Martel said, "you could've told me they were cooking Lotus."

Kid's face turned thoughtful. "Lotus? What makes you say that?"

Martel removed the petals from his coat pocket, letting them flutter to the ground around Kid's feet.

"Just a hunch," Martel replied.

With gray fur and black stripes, Max may not have been the sharpest claw on the paw, but he was big and that's what was important in the Si-Sawat crime syndicate. A Tikarin, a feline race who made up most of Si-Sawat, Max strode through the Fat Cat Casino with a confidence that only brawn and a lack of intelligence could muster. He took in the flashing lights and blaring sounds of the slot machines as he passed through the main floor of the casino.

He had reason to be proud. As the right-hand man of Big G, the head of the syndicate and the betting house, Max had seen the Fat Cat Casino become the biggest and most popular gambling establishment in Regalis. The newly remodeled off-site betting parlor had fifty new screens, showing races and sporting events from all over the planet. More income flowing through the coffers meant the real purpose of the casino, to launder money from Si-Sawat's illicit activities, could continue unabated. Even so, not everything was working as planned. Big G had been irritable of late because the lesser gangs had been making trouble.

Not that Max understood any of that. Mostly he just enjoyed the blinking lights...

Passing through a thick, velvet curtain, Max left the main floor and took the stairs up to Big G's office overlooking the action through a large, two-way mirror. The boss wasn't staring out on his empire, however. He was sitting in a chair, reinforced to carry his girth, behind an expansive desk.

"Hey, boss," Max said in a high falsetto voice, entirely unbefitting his size.

Big G looked up and made a smacking sound with his lips. "I hope you've got some good news."

"'Fraid not, boss," Max replied, making a remorseful face.

Big G's orange fur bristled.

"Figures," he said.

"There was a rumble between the Griefers and the Cyberpunks," Max said.

"A rumble?"

"Yeah, a *fight*," Max said.

"I *know* what a rumble is, Max," Big G replied. "What about it?"

"Seems that the Griefers tore up a Cyberpunk chem lab and then there was a rum-- a fight -- after..."

"What's this world coming to?" Big G lamented. "Fighting is bad for business. Don't these idiots know that?"

Max stared at his boss blankly.

"Well, it *is*," Big G replied. "Why can't people just get along?"

Again, a blank stare.

The boss sighed. "Anyway, what kind of chems were they brewing?"

"Lotus, I hear," Max replied.

Big G threw up his short, chubby arms.

"Of course!" he shouted. "It *had* to be that!"

"That's what I heard..."

"You know," Big G went on, "in my day it was Mad Hatter and LSV, but now it's all synthetic chems and overhead."

"Over what?"

"Overhead, Max!" Big G shouted again. "You could hire a guy to stand on a corner and sell Mad Hatter as easily as you please, but now you've got to rent space for flop houses so Lotus Eaters can lay about, dreaming of a better life!"

"I like naps," Max admitted.

"Of course you do," Big G replied, "We *all* like naps, Max, but we don't sleep through dinner time and second breakfast! A cat's gotta *eat*, you know!"

Max nodded, vaguely aware of his stomach rumbling.

"Alright," Big G said, waving his hand toward the door. "Go and see if you can hear anything else about what happened. Come back when you do..."

"'Kay, boss!" Max replied.

He turned and left with a skip in his step, eager to see what the casino buffet was serving today.

CHAPTER FOUR

Henry Riff had a spring in his step. His posture was only slightly slouching, and he had even managed to pull a comb through his usually unruly hair. All this was thanks to Jessica Doric who, while not professing her love for Henry as he might have otherwise hoped, had in fact suggested that Lord Maycare hadn't spent enough time with him and should take the young man for a spa day. Henry had never been to a spa before, but his imagination ran wild with images of busty women giving him massages and gentle skin treatments.

Maycare, however, had other plans.

"Here we are!" he said as the two exited the gravcar. Before them was a decorative facade that spelled out, in blue tiles, the name *Zahmetli Hamami*.

"What's this?" Henry asked, still wide-eyed with excitement.

"The best Turkish bath in the West End!" Maycare replied.

"Turkish bath?" Henry said.

"That's right, my boy!" Maycare said, slapping Henry on the back. "You're in for a *treat*!"

Instead of a busty woman, an elderly man of Ottoman descent greeted them as they entered. Leading them into an adjacent room, the man motioned for Maycare and Henry to remove their clothing and wrap a towel around their waists while donning plastic slippers.

Henry hesitated, having rarely, if ever, disrobed in front of others.

"Come on, Henry!" Maycare shouted. "Don't be shy, son!"

Henry grinned unconvincingly, and slowly removed his shirt and then the rest of his clothes. Compared to Maycare's tanned, muscular physique, Henry's pale, bony exterior gave the impression he had only eaten ramen noodles most of his life, which, as a matter of fact, he had.

"Do you not lift, Henry?" Maycare asked, a look of genuine concern on his face.

"Lift what?" he replied.

Wearing nothing more than a towel and slippers, the two men passed into a room of white marble where they sat on stone benches along the walls. The air in the room was stiflingly hot and even the benches were exceedingly warm. Henry grew concerned that the heat might seep through the towel and burn his tailbone, among other things. Each breath drew in more of the arid air, baking his lungs like a convection oven. Great beads of sweat rolled down Henry's face, his hair dripping over his eyes.

Convinced he was dying, Henry didn't hear anything at first but realized, through the haze of his sizzling brain, that Maycare was talking.

"Candy keeps bothering me about getting a yacht," Maycare said.

"A what?" Henry muttered weakly.

"You know, a *yacht*."

"What about the *Acaz*?" Henry asked.

"No, no," Maycare went on. "Not a starship! I mean a proper yacht. The kind that floats on water..."

Henry, feeling his spirit leaving him, mumbled, "She's pretty..."

"How would you know?" Maycare asked. "I haven't even picked out the boat yet!"

The Five Families were the major houses of the Imperial aristocracy, tracing their lineage directly to the five surviving ark captains that brought humans to Andromeda. Of this handful of families, House Veber often served as kingmakers. While the Augustus and Montros families stood together on one side and the Tagus and Groen families stood on the other, the Vebers remained in the middle, unaffiliated with the others. For this reason, with his father's abdication imminent, Prince Richard found himself at the Veber estate in the West End of Regalis. He had come to speak with the matriarch of the family, Lady Rebecca Veber.

He was not looking forward to the conversation.

Lady Veber spent much of her time away from the capital on a planet called Lokeren. However, as it happened, she was currently residing at her estate on Aldorus, saving Richard the trip. Richard was not sure whether he should be thankful for this, since he had less time to prepare what he was going to say.

One of Lady Veber's servants greeted the prince in the atrium.

The servant bowed and led the prince up a white-marble staircase and through a pair of double doors painted a light blue. Inside, Lady Veber reclined on a chaise lounge, the legs carved from ivory. In her mid-forties with a wide face and blue eyes, she wore her blond hair in an intricate braid.

Standing as Prince Richard entered, she straightened the aqua taffeta of her long gown.

"Your Royal Majesty," she said. "What brings you to my *humble* home?"

The prince gave the servant a side eye, prompting Lady Veber to shoo him away.

"There's something important we have to discuss," Richard said once the servant had gone.

"Considering how long it's been since the *last time* you've visited me," Lady Veber replied with bite in her tone, "it *must* be something important."

"I apologize," the prince said. "I know it's been a while."

"If memory serves me," she went on, "it was sometime shortly before your father had me institutionalized."

Prince Richard winced before clearing his throat.

"It was a regrettable circumstance," he said, "but to be fair, you had just murdered the head of the Tagus family."

"The man who *killed* my son!" Lady Veber shouted, her face suddenly red.

Richard took a breath before answering.

"Be that as it may," he said slowly, "the Emperor showed mercy when he allowed you to recover from your grief in seclusion instead of having you *executed*."

Lady Veber sighed.

"The grounds of the Regency Heights Sanatorium were indeed lovely," she said more calmly. "I enjoyed feeding the ducks by the lake..."

"The past is the past," Richard went on. "I'm here to talk about the present and the future."

"Yes?"

"My father has decided to abdicate."

"I beg your pardon?" Lady Veber replied, her meticulously groomed eyebrows raised.

"The announcement is imminent," the prince continued, "but I wanted to speak with you first."

Lady Veber sat back on the couch. Her reddened face had turned an ashen pale.

"You realize what Rupert will do if he's selected as the next emperor," she said, referring to the current head of the Tagus family.

"Considering that you killed his father," Richard replied, "I suspect you will not escape execution after all."

Lady Veber's eyes fixed on the prince. Slowly, she nodded.

Roland entered the same alley that Gregor Ivanovich had exited previously. Lefty Lucy had given him directions on how to get there and, with the purple card tucked between his fingers, Roland felt the confines of the alley folding in around him as he left the main street.

Roland stopped when he came to an image of an angry face painted on the wall that matched the one on the card. Just as Lucy had told him, Roland placed his palm against the face until the lines started to glow. A section of the wall retracted and slid away, exposing a passageway, the faint scent of jasmine wafting out into the alley.

After hesitating for a moment, Roland followed the corridor down a slight incline, until it opened into a large chamber filled with expensive rugs and tapestries. A man in a dark robe with gold trim lay on a bed of pillows. Beside him stood a woman, also in robes, with green skin and a respirator covering most of her face. Both were bald, with circuitry interwoven across their scalps.

What the hell am I doing here? Roland thought.

Don't worry, someone said directly into Roland's mind. *We won't bite.*

The man laughed.

"Sorry," he said. "I couldn't resist."

Getting to his feet, he approached Roland with an outstretched hand. "My name is Kanet Solan and this is my colleague, Ta Demona."

Roland shook Solan's hand, the skin cold, almost unnatural. He speculated how much of the man was actually machine before realizing Solan could obviously read minds.

"Quite a lot," Solan replied with a frown. "Do you know who we are, boy?"

"My mother said you were the Psi Lords," Roland said.

"Your *adopted* mother, you mean?" he replied. "Yes, Lefty Lucy was quite right. As it happens, you can thank *her* for this audience. We owed her a small favor..."

"Thank you for seeing me," the boy said.

"I assure you," Solan went on, "if we meet again, it will be *you* who owes *us* a favor."

"I understand."

"Do you?" Solan asked. "As Lucy may have told you, we are a data cartel. We deal in information, which is presumably why you are here. However, this comes at a price."

"I don't have any money," Roland admitted.

"Of course not," Solan said, "but we can come to an arrangement nevertheless."

"What does that mean?"

"It means, as I've already said, you will owe us a favor. At some point you will hear from us and you must do as we say."

"I can fight," Roland said.

Solan's mouth curled into a sneer.

"Any fool can fight," he replied. "I hope you'll be more useful than *that*."

"I'll do what I need to do."

"Yes, you will," Solan said.

In the Turkish bath, two large men, both bald and each wearing a white t-shirt and shorts, appeared through a second door and ushered Henry and Maycare to follow them into another room, this one octagon shaped. In the center was a marble platform raised two feet off the ground. Arches, supported by slender columns, ran around the circumference of the room along with water basins protruding from the walls.

Without prompting, Maycare removed his slippers and towel and laid face down, naked on the platform. Henry required a great deal more prompting. One of the large Turkish men pointed at Henry's towel and then the dais. Growing impatient, he slapped his sizable hands together in a loud clap.

Henry jumped at the sound and removed what little cover he wore before reluctantly lying down beside Maycare.

On the hot slab of marble, Henry felt the rough, firm hands of the man on his pale, fragile shoulders. The man was not a gentleman.

The masseur's coarse fingers dug between Henry's shoulder blades before grasping one of his scrawny arms and bending it backwards. Naked and very much afraid, Henry absorbed the punishment, feeling more pain than relaxation.

Who would enjoy this? Henry wondered.

"This feels *great*!" Maycare shouted. "Really loosens the muscles!"

After a final sound of his bones cracking, Henry felt a thunderous slap on his behind.

"Alright, Henry," Maycare said, getting back to his feet. "Wash yourself off."

Feeling like a cat at the dog park, Henry had never been more relieved to be leaving. Stumbling to one of the basins against the wall, he cupped his hands and dumped cold water over his face. He had to admit, the chilling liquid was refreshing. He followed Maycare into yet another room where robes and fresh slippers awaited them. Once again at least partially clothed, the two men entered a lounge area with wooden deck chairs and tables where servantbots brought tea for them to drink.

Lying in the chair, Henry closed his eyes and took deep breaths, hoping the pain throughout his body would fade as quickly as the memories of a strange man pummeling him.

"Devlin, ol' buddy!" a voice said loudly.

Henry cracked an eye open and saw a man about the same age as Maycare approaching. He wore the same robe and slippers as everyone else, but also a panama hat.

"Ducky!" Maycare shouted. "How the hell are you?"

The two shook hands, while Maycare remained sitting. Henry shut his eyes again but listened attentively.

"Good to see you walking around," Ducky said.

"Well, of course," Maycare said. "You can't keep a good man down!"

"I mean, I heard about your accident," Ducky clarified.

"That was no accident," Maycare replied.

"No?"

"Somebody sabotaged my sled! If I ever get my hands on whoever's responsible..."

"Any suspects?" Ducky asked.

"I had assumed it was Grayson," Maycare replied, "but he swears up and down he's innocent."

"And you believe him?"

"He gave his word as a gentleman."

"Well, that's ironclad then," Ducky replied.

Henry couldn't tell if he was being ironic or not.

"I'm thinking about hiring someone to look into it," Maycare said.

"A detective?"

"I suppose so," Maycare replied, "but it would have to be somebody trustworthy."

"As it happens," Henry heard Ducky say, "I may know a guy who knows a guy..."

"Well, that would be outstanding!" Maycare replied. "You were always a man with connections, Ducky."

Henry opened his eyes. Ducky was smiling and using the panama hat to fan himself.

"It pays to know people," Ducky said with a wink.

Kanet Solan offered Roland a seat, namely a large cushion on the floor. Incense sticks, stuck in bowls of sand on a nearby table, sent coils of smoke undulating around the boy's head.

Solan, taking a pillow beside Roland, casually tapped the table with an unusually long fingernail.

"I wonder," the Psi Lord said, "what do you know about how you and Lucy first met?"

The teenager adjusted himself on top of the pillow but found it uncomfortable. He would have preferred a chair.

"Just what she told me," he replied. "A man named Pitt brought me to her when I was still a baby."

"*Pitt*, you say?" Solan asked. "Not much to go on..."

"My mom said he worked for military intelligence," Roland went on, "although I guess he was a pirate before that."

Solan's eyes widened. "Lucy knew a pirate?"

"My mom had a colorful background before she became a bodyguard for Prince Alexander."

"Indeed!" Solan said. "And that's when she originally met this Pitt fellow?"

"I guess," Roland replied, shrugging, "but he doesn't go by Pitt anymore."

"Why is that?"

"I guess whatever made him bring me to Lucy meant he had to leave the military," Roland said. "He laid low after that..."

Solan started tapping the table again. "Interesting."

"Can you help me?" Roland asked finally.

The tapping stopped.

"Oh, I imagine we can," Solan said, "but the real question is, can *you* help *us*?"

"I promised I'll do whatever needs doing," Roland replied in earnest.

Solan smiled, his grin making Roland even more uncomfortable than the pillows.

"*Pacta sunt servanda*," Solan said.

"What?" the boy asked.

"Agreements must be kept," the Psi Lord replied. "It's the very basis of business and this is, after all, a business."

Collecting his courage, Roland held out his hand. "So, do we have an agreement?"

Solan's grin widened, raising the hair on Roland's neck. Once again, he felt the cold skin of the Psi Lord's palm touch his own.

"Indeed, we do," Solan replied, shaking the boy's hand.

Like his father the Emperor, Prince Richard Augustus lived in the Imperial Palace. While not as luxurious as the Emperor's quarters, Richard's apartment occupied an entire wing and, compared to the tenements of Ashetown, was not too shabby.

Richard arrived home after the long day, greeted by his wife at the door.

Lady Lilith Augustus gave her husband a quick peck on the cheek. Maneuvering around his wife's sizable baby bump, Richard returned the favor.

Although she was eight months pregnant, Lilith still appeared thin and frail. Her smile, like the rest of her face, was restrained and her brown hair, hanging just past her shoulders, was slightly curled on the ends. She wore diamond earrings, not large but just large enough that a crowd could see them from a distance. As a rule, people did not call her Lilly or Lil. They all referred to her as Lady Lilith, except perhaps her husband, and then only just.

They moved to the parlor where a butlerbot had left a tray with tiny sandwiches and a large glass of bourbon. Richard ignored the former and took a long drink from the latter.

"Hard day?" Lilith asked, reclining on a teal, Louis XV sofa.

In his own chair, Richard placed the nearly empty glass back on the table. "And then some."

"What happened?" she asked.

"My father wants to abdicate," Richard replied grimly.

"What?" Lilith said. "So soon?"

"Not soon enough, according to my father."

Lilith's narrow mouth tightened further. "I know he's not getting any younger, but he's hardly decrepit..."

"True," Richard agreed. "He still has his wits about him, but he thinks the time is right."

"Our baby will be born in a month," Lilith scoffed. "The Emperor really wants our child born into the turmoil of an Imperial Conclave?"

Richard eyed the bourbon remaining in the glass but left it alone.

"The conclave will decide the new emperor, whether our baby is born or not," he said. "My father thinks the rest of the Imperium is peaceful enough that it's now or never. Personally, I would have preferred he considered his own family at least as much as the rest of the Empire."

"Perhaps you could speak to him?"

"What do you think I've been doing?" Richard snapped at his wife.

"I don't like your tone, Richard!" she replied fiercely.

He sighed. "Sorry, my dear."

"At any rate," she went on, "who do you think will be selected as the new emperor?"

"It all depends on whom each of the Five Families favors most," Richard replied. "My fear is that it could be Rupert Tagus, but it can't be someone from *my* family. That much is certain."

Although not from the Five Families, Lilith came from one of the many secondary houses of the aristocracy. Nevertheless, she retained all the pride and cunning of the primary five. Richard could see the wheels working in her head.

"What if it wasn't?" she asked finally.

"Wasn't what?" he replied.

"What if *you* could be declared emperor?"

"You know that's not possible," Richard said. "None of the Five Families can rule consecutively as Emperor."

"Where is that written?" she asked. "What law says that's the case?"

"Well," Richard said, "it's always been the tradition. The families simply adhere to it by mutual agreement..."

"What if the agreement was no longer *mutual?*" Lilith said.

Seeing that his wife was deadly serious, Richard took the glass from the table and downed the remaining bourbon. He knew that look and knew what it could mean.

Summers in Regalis could be hot, and this one was no different. However, stretched out in a deckchair on a pleasure yacht, Lord Radford Groen felt a cooling breeze coming off the Regalis River. The boat, christened the *Rey Sol*, was not his. That honor belonged to Lord Devlin Maycare who graciously had invited Groen for a day of lounging while the yacht remained anchored along the riverbank.

With West End off the port bow and Middleton off the starboard, Ashetown was somewhere to the stern, out of sight and out of mind. Groen rested in his chair, staring at the sky and a hovering advertisement that read:

DO YOU LOVE THE TASTE OF PORK
BUT HATE ALL THE CHEWING?
SAY HELLO TO HALLO, HAM-FLAVORED JELLO!
ANOTHER QUALITY PRODUCT FROM MOFOCO!

Come to think of it, Groen thought, *I do enjoy the taste of pork...*

"What are you thinking about?" Maycare asked from the chair beside him. Dressed in swim trunks and wearing dark shades, Maycare lay with his bare chest soaking up the sun.

"Huh? Oh, nothing," Groen replied, also in trunks. He felt a buzzing under his leg and pulled a datapad out from beneath him.

"What is it?" Maycare asked.

Groen surveyed the screen and laughed.

"I won another race!" he said.

Maycare pulled off his sunglasses and gave an approving glance. "Well done, Radford!"

"I'm on the best winning streak of my life!" he replied.

"If you don't mind me saying," Maycare went on, "you were right to get Winnie Woodwick out of your life. He was nothing but bad luck!"

Groen tucked the datapad back under his leg.

"I think you're right," he said. "All this time I thought it was me, but really, Winnie was the problem."

"Agreed," Maycare replied.

From below deck, Lady Candice Woodwick appeared in a bright pink bikini and pink sunglasses. Her flowing blond hair caught the river breeze, twirling around her bare shoulders.

"Ahoy, boys!" she shouted.

Both men smiled.

"About time, Candy," Maycare remarked. "You'll never get a tan down in the cabin..."

Candy approached the deck chairs, stopping beside Groen's.

"Never you mind that," she said, bending to kiss Groen on the lips.

Maycare's eyes widened and he jumped to his feet. "What the hell, Candy?"

"Don't make a scene, Devlin sweetheart," she replied, "but I've decided to leave you for Radford."

"What? Is this true?" Maycare asked Groen.

"The heart wants what the heart wants," Groen replied graciously. "I hope you'll understand."

Maycare threw his sunglasses aside. "No, I certainly *do not*!"

Groen got to his feet as well, gently pushing Candy out of harm's way. Maycare lunged, taking a wide swing at Groen's chin. Missing, he stumbled forward while Groen landed a punch of his own into Maycare's ribs.

Maycare let out a loud grunt. Collecting himself, he took another swing which again missed the mark. Groen countered with an uppercut which landed on Maycare's sizable jaw. Stunned, Maycare was unprepared for Groen's next attack, a spinning kick that landed in the yacht owner's stomach.

Maycare fell backwards and tumbled over the railing. Candy screamed.

"I'm sorry you had to see that," Groen said, attempting to calm her. "I promise I'll make it up to you."

"How?" she asked.

"Why don't we go back to the cabin and I'll show you?" he replied.

Before Candy could respond, Groen felt a tug at his swim trunks and realized Maycare was hanging on the outside of the railing with one hand and dragging him closer with the other. With a strong pull, Groen toppled over the side of the boat, falling into the river. With a splash, Groen's body sank like a stone, the water swirling around him. Fighting to breathe, he thrashed with his arms and legs, but the current surrounded him like ropes, binding him and pulling him deeper. Groen gasped and realized he was wrapped in silk sheets.

He woke in his bed, Lord Woodwick standing beside him in their shared apartment.

"I say, Radford!" Woodwick said with alarm, "it's about time you got up!"

In a fog, Groen tried somewhat unsuccessfully to untangle himself. "What's going on?"

"You've been in bed all day," Woodwick replied. "You've completely slept through teatime!"

"Where's Devlin?" Groen asked. "And Candy?"

"My niece?" Woodwick said. "I suppose they're off gallivanting somewhere... Why in heaven's name would you want to know that?"

Groen stopped struggling and laid back in bed.

"No reason," he said.

"Are you still eating those petals Ducky gave you?" Woodwick asked.

Groen closed his eyes.

"No," he lied, wishing he was still asleep.

CHAPTER FIVE

Gregor Ivanovich and his gang, the Cyberpunks, were setting fire to a warehouse owned by the Griefers. In one corner, Gregor found something odd. Nailed by its fluffy ear to a wooden post, the decapitated head of a stuffed toy hung about three feet off the ground. Just above the teddy bear's head, crudely carved by a knife, were the words:

THE GREAT
TUBBY WUBBY
MASSACRE

With his newly installed eye, Gregor scanned the head and found it was filled with electronics and, most surprisingly, a synthetic brain. Superimposed in his line of sight, Gregor saw the word "Abnormal" flashing next to the outline of the brain.

The gangster held a sword in his hand. Instead of metal, the blade was a shaft of plasma, flames flickering along its length. Gregor pressed the tip of the plasma sword against the stuffed head and watched it catch fire. The bear's eyes opened and it said, "I'll cut you," before the flames consumed it entirely.

Two days before he and the rest of his gang were setting fire to the Griefer warehouse, Gregor was touring one of his own properties. As the leader of the Cyberpunks, Gregor kept tabs on the various businesses serving as fronts for the gang's otherwise illicit activities.

On that day he was visiting a laundromat . Mostly automated, the shop took in clothing at the front, but through a door in the back, Gregor entered a much larger establishment. He nodded at a pair of his men guarding the door and passed into a long hallway with doors on either side. He pushed a door open and peered into a darkened room full of mattresses lying on the floor. On these makeshift beds, men and women were sprawled out in various positions, some flat on their backs while others were curled into balls. To the casual observer, they appeared dead, but from the sounds of snoring, Gregor knew his customers were very much alive.

At the end of the hall, he stepped into yet another room. This one contained tables instead of bedding, and members of his gang preparing trays of Lotus petals to be distributed to the sleepers when they eventually awoke. The Lotus den didn't provide food or drink, and the customers never asked for any. Occasionally, as a public service, one of the gangsters would force an addict to go eat something, but before long, the Lotus Eater was back for another round of slumber. The dreams were too enticing to ignore.

Gregor liked what he saw, but as he turned back down the hall leading to the laundromat at the front, one of his gang approached. He wore heavy boots and a long waistcoat, a long sleeveless jacket that hung past his waist. He had marks on the side of his face, as if he had been peppered with fragments, the blood now dried into streaks of brown.

"What happened?" Gregor asked.

"They hit the chem lab!" the gangster replied.

"Where's Alexei?"

"They killed him."

"Who did?" Gregor asked, already knowing answer.

"Griefers," the man replied. "Mr. Munge and some guy with a big gun!"

Gregor's fingers tightened into a fist.

The leather couch in Martel's office was already old when he bought it used. The brown hide had faded in places and was scarred from dropped cigarettes. On the other hand, it was surprisingly comfortable to sleep on and, seeing how he lacked any other residence, Martel used the couch as a bed most nights. On this particular morning, he woke with the sun blinding his eyes.

"Ugh," he groaned, shading his face with the back of his hand. Martel pulled himself into a seated position, his bare feet on the wooden floor. He had a particular taste in his mouth, somewhere between acrid smoke and rye whiskey. He crossed the room to a sink in the corner and wondered if he had paid the water bill that month. To Martel's surprise, the tap still worked so he splashed his face, drying it with a questionable hand towel.

Martel dressed in a pair of pants and an undershirt before stepping into the front of the office where Dolores immediately assaulted him with her Long Island accent.

"Did ja hear the news, hon?" she began, her voice coming from the box on the desk.

"You know I just got up, right?" Martel replied sourly.

"Get some cawffee then, suga, and listen to this!" she said.

From the same box came a different voice, which Martel recognized as Sylvia Flax, the anchor for VOX News.

"In a stunning announcement," Flax said, "Emperor Augustus has declared he will abdicate the throne! It's unclear when his Imperial Majesty will be stepping down, but all will depend on when an Imperial Conclave can convene and pick his successor."

"Isn't that exciting?" Dolores' voice returned.

"Sure," Martel replied dryly.

"I don't know about you, but I think it's important!"

The detective remained skeptical.

"The goings on in West End don't matter much here in Ashetown," he said. "Emperors come and go, but the poor stay poor..."

"Well, ain't you a Grumpy Gus!" Dolores remarked. "Anyhow, yawr lady friend called."

"Lady friend?" Martel asked.

"Sure, the one from Wawlock Industries..."

"You mean Dr. Sprouse?"

"Yeah," Dolores said. "Anyways, yawr *doctor* lady friend said she's analyzed the petals you sent her."

"Already?" Martel replied. "Have her meet me at the Sous-Sol..."

"She already said she wouldn't be cawt dead in a dump like that."

"Fine," Martel muttered with a sigh. "Tell her to pick a place then."

"Will do, chief!"

The rumpled detective turned toward the back room.

"Goin' back to bed?" Dolores asked.

"No," Martel replied. "I've got to work for a living..."

Gregor Ivanovich had been a sickly child. His father called him a weakling, mocking the boy's pasty skin and dark, sunken eyes. As Gregor grew older, bullies in the neighborhood picked on him relentlessly and he often returned home bruised and angry. He fell in with other disenfranchised youths, each carrying their own grudges against the society that had rejected them. It was particularly galling that humans were the favored race of the Imperium, yet other humans looked at Gregor and his gang brothers with disdain and fear.

Sometime during his late teens, Gregor noticed an automated blimp passing over the slums he called home. An advertisement ran across the balloon:

THE WORLD IS YOURS
FOR 3 EASY PAYMENTS
OF 19.95!

Gregor didn't remember what the ad was for but it hardly mattered. He saw in those words a call to action.

I promise, he told himself, *I will never be weak again!*

However, even though Gregor founded his own gang, other gangs like the Griefers remained dominant in Ashetown, often at Gregor's expense. It was only after the robot revolution five years ago that things finally changed.

Alexei, Gregor's right-hand man, watched the signing of the Cyber Civil Liberties Bill on the news at the time.

"What's it all mean, boss?" he asked.

"I'm not sure," Gregor replied, "but I think we're about to become obsolete..."

In the Imperium, at least among humans, purity was everything. The very fabric of the nobility was based on their ability to trace a direct line to the crews of the ark ships that had brought humanity to Andromeda. Even the middle class spoke with pride of their ancestors, the colonists who had slept in suspended animation for the entire trip. Humans viewed their DNA as a sacred code, making genetic alterations an abomination. Even a prosthesis, beyond a simple artificial arm or leg, was taboo, leading to Imperial laws and decrees banning mechanical and cybernetic augmentation.

Gregor realized this was a limitation.

Robots were smarter and stronger than fleshlings, and Gregor was not about to be left behind. Within months, he began outfitting his gang, and himself, with augmentations. From brain enhancements to internal weapons systems, the newly renamed *Cyberpunks* suddenly became a force to be reckoned with.

The sun had just disappeared behind the skyscrapers of Middleton, the business district of Regalis, when Thomas Martel met his contact, Dr. Sprouse, at a small park surrounded by glass and concrete buildings. She sat on a bench alone, her bright red hair still vibrant, even in the fading light. Although she wore a light jacket, her lab coat with the logo of Warlock Industries was still visible underneath.

"You thought this was better than the Sous-Sol?" Martel asked, taking a seat beside her.

"A burning garbage fire would be better than the Sous-Sol," she replied curtly.

Martel crossed his arms. "Thanks for meeting me anyway."

From her coat, the doctor pulled out the plastic evidence bag filled with the petals that Martel had taken at the Cyberpunk chem lab. She slipped it into Martel's lap.

"It's Lotus," she said.

Taking the bag, Martel rolled his eyes. "I knew that already. What else can you tell me?"

"It's a synthetic narcotic," Sprouse said, "based on a toxic fungus spore."

"A fungus?"

"On the planet Eudora Prime," she went on, "there's a creature -- a walking plant actually -- that produces a cloud of poisonous spores to defend itself. It's called the *Kamal Maut*."

Martel gave her a blank look.

"It means Death Lotus," she said, shaking her head.

"Ah," Martel replied. "And somebody made it into a chem?"

"Apparently."

"I heard it makes people have crazy dreams," he said.

"Correct," Sprouse replied. "It affects the parts of the brain that influence sleep and the dream state. It's also highly addictive."

From down the sidewalk, a park patrolbot rolled laboriously toward them. About four feet tall and shaped like a cone on little wheels, it stopped in front of the bench. A small hatch opened along the robot's surface and a prong-like rod with two electrodes extended out, pointing at Martel. Small bolts of electricity jumped between the prongs.

"Is this vagrant bothering you, Ma'am?" the patrolbot asked.

Sprouse pondered a moment. "A little."

The probe with the electrodes extended farther, drawing dangerously close to Martel's leg.

"Hey!" the detective shouted. "I'm not a vagrant! I *have* a job!"

The pale blue eye of the robot stared at Martel.

"If you say so," it replied.

"I'm fine," Sprouse said to the robot. "You can go."

The patrolbot made a chirping noise and retracted the probe. Turning, it went about its business down the sidewalk.

"Thanks," Martel said.

"It serves you right," Sprouse remarked. "You can't expect me to run lab tests whenever you like."

"You owed me a favor," Martel said.

"Then consider it paid," she replied. "Warlock Industries doesn't pay me to do your dirty work."

"No, they pay you to do *their* dirty work..."

"Damn right," the doctor said. "Are we done here?"

"I mean," Martel replied, not entirely finished, "how do you sleep at night, knowing all the terrible things Warlock does?"

Doctor Sprouse stood while giving the detective a smile. "Very well," she said and walked away.

Gregor Ivanovich did not attack immediately. He carefully weighed Griefer targets before choosing one warehouse in particular, containing the gang's most valuable merchandise. While not a crippling blow to Kid Vicious, the counterattack would cost the Griefers millions in potential profits.

Just past sunset, the Cyberpunks overwhelmed the warehouse guards, killing them, and then turned their attention to the storage crates, setting them on fire.

"This is for Alexei!" Gregor shouted, holding the flaming plasma sword in his hand.

The Griefers staged their own counterattack before the warehouse was completely ablaze. Armed with blasters and guns, they streamed into the burning building, the sound of shots and crackling fire filling the air.

Kid Vicious himself, his pants ironically painted with flames, appeared amongst the choking smoke.

"You crazy son-of-a-bitch!" he shouted at Gregor from across the warehouse floor. "I'm going to wipe you out for this!"

With a blaster in each hand, he fired at the Cyberpunk leader. Gregor ducked behind a container, the blaster bolts turning the sides into melted plastic.

Gregor poked his head out.

"Give it up, Kid!" he yelled back. "You're no match against our augmentations. Your time has come and *gone!*"

Through his X-ray eye, Gregor noticed the shape of a Griefer approaching on the other side of the container. Wearing a red leather jacket and carrying a shotgun, the man appeared around the corner, leveling the barrel of the gun.

Gregor sliced it in half with his plasma sword, taking the Griefer's left arm along with it. The man screamed in pain but stopped abruptly as Gregor decapitated him with another swing of the sword.

Gregor smiled, but forgot about Kid who had used the opportunity to close the gap between the two gang leaders. When Gregor turned, Kid was waiting with his blasters.

"Augmentations are no substitute for experience," Kid said, pointing the blasters while flames blazed above him in the rafters.

"But before I kill you," he went on, "who's been bankrolling your expansion?"

Gregor dropped his sword to the ground. "I don't know what you mean..."

"You don't have the capital for all that Lotus," Kid replied. "Somebody with deep pockets has been supplying you with chems."

"Like I said," Gregor replied calmly, "you're outdated and people have noticed."

"Which people?"

"People who see the future and recognize you're not in it!" Gregor replied.

Something exploded above them, followed by a burning wooden beam crashing down. Both Gregor and Kid scrambled out of the way, the rafter landing between them. Gregor rolled across the floor until he felt the cold metal of his sword's hilt in his hands. At the same time, blaster streaks cut through the smoke. With his enhanced vision, Gregor could clearly see Kid on the other side of the flames, firing blindly.

Once more, Gregor could not help but grin.

Idiot, he thought. *Let him burn...*

Crawling away, Gregor notified his men via their communication implants to leave as well. The warehouse was fully engulfed, but this was only the beginning.

The gang war had just begun.

Martel took a gravtaxi from Middleton back to Ashetown. After paying the robot driver and stepping onto the cracked cement of the sidewalk, Martel caught a whiff of smoke in the air. His eyes surveyed the run-down buildings around him which were in stark contrast to the business towers of Middleton. The low clouds had turned pink, reflecting a raging fire several blocks away. A thick column of smoke trailed into the sky like a portent of bad times ahead.

That can't be good, he thought.

The detective bypassed the stairs down to the Sous-Sol, taking the flight up to his office instead.

"Yawr back!" Dolores said as Martel walked through the door. "How was yawr lady docta friend?"

"Just dandy," he replied, passing directly into the back and taking a seat at this desk. He pulled the plastic bag out of his jacket, holding it up to the light. The thin petals inside the bag were semi-translucent.

Opening a drawer, he shoved the pouch inside, happy he wasn't an addict like those poor bastards in the Lotus dens. From the same drawer, he removed a bottle and a shot glass.

He poured a drink and emptied it in a single gulp before pouring another.

"Ya gotta call comin' in, hon!" Dolores shouted from the other room.

Now? Martel thought.

He grabbed a datapad from the desk, pushing the bottle and glass just out of view.

"Okay!" he yelled.

Dolores transferred the call to the pad in Martel's hand. The face of a remarkably handsome man appeared on the screen.

"Hello!" the man said. "I'm Lord Devlin Maycare."

"I'm Detective Thomas Martel. What can I do for you?"

"Ducky Davenport said I should give you a call..." Maycare replied.

"I don't think I know anybody named *Ducky*," Martel admitted.

"Maybe so, but he knows *you*!" Maycare said. "I'm in need of a private eye and he told me you're the man I should call."

Martel finally recognized the face on the screen. "You're that famous sportsman, Lord Maycare."

Maycare grinned with the kind of feigned humility only a professional athlete could muster.

"Why, yes," he said. "You've seen me play?"

"I've caught a few of your races," Martel remarked.

"Well, that's why I'm calling," Maycare went on. "Of course, it's a matter of some delicacy. It requires absolute discretion."

"Discretion is my specialty," the detective replied.

"In fact, I'd prefer to give you the details in person."

"You could come to my office in Ashetown."

Maycare stifled a laugh at the thought. "Actually, I'd prefer you came to my estate in West End."

"Your estate?" Martel asked.

"Yes," Maycare said. "It's a big house. You can't miss it..."

"Right," the detective replied. "I'm sure I can find it."

"Capital!" Maycare shouted, obviously pleased. "Say, tomorrow afternoon around one?"

"I'll be there."

Maycare's smiling face winked into a blank screen. Martel, for his part, made a noise deep in his throat and reached for the bottle. He poured a drink into the shot glass and downed it, wondering if he still had a clean tie to wear.

As part of the expansion of the Fat Cat Casino, Big G had built an adjacent luxury hotel, although the term *luxury* was somewhat generous. Big G had grand designs for his hotel, including gold inlays and draperies of crimson velvet. Once he learned the cost of such amenities, however, he chose gilded bronze and red velour instead. Even so, his own personal penthouse at the top of the building did not lack luxury, and Big G could feel some satisfaction in that at least.

In the sunken living room of the suite, Big G lay on his back while a servantbot gently stroked the Tikarin's fur with a brush. The soft bristles passed through his mane, eliciting purrs from the criminal kingpin.

"Yeah, that's what I'm talking about," Big G murmured, his thick neck rippling.

The robot paused to remove some of the orange hair from the brush.

"Are you stressed?" he asked. "You're losing more hair than usual."

"That figures," Big G replied. "Heavy is the head that wears the crown..."

A metal door slid apart revealing an elevator and Max, Big G's right-hand man, within. The large feline lumbered into the penthouse with a glum expression.

"What's the matter, Max?" his boss asked. "Can't you ever bring me any *good* news?"

"Sorry," Max replied in his surprisingly high voice. "I would if I could."

The gangster stepped down into the living room as Big G motioned for the servantbot to continue brushing.

"I didn't tell you to stop," he told the robot. Turning to Max, he asked, "Did Radford Groen ask for another extension on what he owes me?"

"No, boss," Max replied. "I haven't seen him in a week."

"What?" Big G sat up, genuinely surprised. "He better not be spending his money someplace else!"

Max shook his head. "It ain't about him, boss. There's trouble with the street gangs."

"Which ones?"

"The Griefers and the Cyberpunks."

"I knew it!" Big G shouted, causing the robot to let go of the brush which hung loosely in Big G's back fur.

"Those two idiots!" Big G went on, barely aware of what was going on behind him. "Ivanovich and the Kid don't have two brain cells to rub between them..."

"Yeah, boss," Max replied, not a rocket scientist himself.

"What did they do this time?" Big G asked.

"The Cyberpunks attacked a Griefer warehouse and set it on fire."

"Which one?"

"The big one on Dashiell Street," Max replied.

"Kid Vicious must be losing his mind," Big G remarked.

"He was there. Both him and Gregor had it out, I heard."

"Well, I hope at least one of them got killed."

"Neither, boss," Max said. "They're both alive."

Big G waved off the servant bot who had only just retrieved the brush.

"You realize what this means?" Big G asked his enforcer.

"You're done gettin' brushed?" Max replied.

"No, you big dummy," his boss said. "It means a gang war in Ashetown!"

"That don't sound good."

Big G stared at Max like a parent explaining something to a child.

"No," the boss said. "It doesn't sound good at *all*."

CHAPTER SIX

On video monitors across the city of Regalis, the smiling face of Sylvia Flax appeared from the studios of VOX News. Her long, azure hair hanging past her shoulders, Flax was the face billions in the Imperium depended on to deliver the news, good or bad.

"Thank you for joining us," she began in a firm, resolved voice. "Yesterday, the Imperial Palace announced Emperor Augustus would be stepping down. Today, the emperor himself will address the people of the Imperium, brought to you by Max Jō Coffee."

Words were superimposed across the anchor's face:

MAX Jō
EXTREME COFFEE:
SLEEP WHEN YOU'RE DEAD!

Just below the main text of the advertisement, in print so small it was barely visible, were the words "Warning: May cause premature death."

"Nobody knows what Emperor Augustus will say in his speech," Flax continued as the ad slowly faded, "but many must wonder what this will mean for the Imperium. Who will be the next Emperor or Empress, and how long before we find out?"

Like the advertisement, Flax's own face disappeared, replaced with that of the emperor as he sat behind an impressive desk trimmed with gold. On his bald head, he wore the formal Imperial crown, a jeweled splendor of diamonds, rubies, and various other precious gems. Behind him hung the flags of the Imperium and the Augustus family, flanking a window overlooking the palace gardens.

Augustus stared into the camera for a moment, holding the collective attention of millions, and billions once the speech was eventually transmitted across the empire. When he finally spoke, his voice was hoarse, perhaps showing his age.

"People of the Imperium," he said, "I have had the great pleasure of being your Emperor for many years. During that period, I have guided you through times of war and times of peace, times of recession and times of prosperity. In all my years as emperor, however, I have always kept the good of the Imperium above all else. It is with that in mind that I announce my abdication."

Pausing for effect, the emperor continued.

"I have called on the Five Families to assemble a conclave to decide who will next wear the crown. Until a decision has been made, I will remain your emperor and your humble servant. Long live the Imperium!"

The video feed returned to Sylvia Flax who, instinctively, took a breath.

"Well, there you have it," she said, exhaling, "a momentous announcement by Emperor Augustus that will undoubtedly shape the Imperium for years to come, again, brought to you by Max Jō."

While the ad for extreme coffee replayed, a recording of the event was already transmitting at the speed of light to a data satellite elsewhere in the Aldorus star system. From there, courier drones carried the emperor's address across the empire, distributing its message from system to system, from planet to planet, until everyone eventually knew that the man who had been their emperor for most of their lives would soon be replaced by someone new. While many, especially at the fringes of the Imperium, would shrug and go about their daily lives, a select few in the capital were thrown into action. For them, this was an opportunity of a lifetime and they would not let it go to waste.

In the West End, not far from the main thoroughfare called Embassy Row, the Emissary Hotel catered to a rich clientele of diplomats and ambassadors as well as the local nobility. The hotel featured a restaurant called *The Grove*, decorated with palm trees and other tropical plants. While the Grove served breakfast, lunch, and dinner, its most popular meal was brunch for those unable to get up for breakfast, but too famished to wait for lunch.

Two such people were Lady Lilith Augustus and Lady Candice Woodwick. Their table, on a raised tier overlooking the main floor of the restaurant, had an excellent view of the other patrons eating from their plates of crêpes, croissants, and avocado toast.

Lilith wore a tightly fitting green dress with gold buttons over her baby bump while Candy's attire was far more casual, a black and white striped jacket with a pink top underneath. To the casual observer, these two seemed an unlikely pair. However, having gone to the same finishing school as girls, they had become fast friends and remained so ever since.

"I don't believe it," Lilith said, her restrained face almost showing emotion. "Rupert Tagus is over there with Lady Veber..."

Candy, having just tried her poached egg, started to turn before Lady Augustus stopped her.

"Don't look!" she hissed through clenched teeth. "Okay, *now* look!"

Peering over her shoulder, Candy saw Lord Rupert Tagus III sharing a table across the room with the matriarch of the Veber family, Lady Rebecca Veber.

Candy waited to speak until she swallowed. "I wonder what they're talking about?"

"What do you think?" Lilith replied in her usual, scolding tone. "They must be discussing the conclave."

"Really?" Candy replied.

"They're both voting members of their families," Lilith went on, "and it's Lady Veber's vote that usually breaks a tie."

"But I thought Lady Veber hated the Taguses?"

"Of course! They killed her son!"

"Right," Candy replied before taking another bite.

"But Rupert is cunning," Lilith said. "He must have something up his sleeve if he's talking with her like this."

"Who is the Augustus family voting for?" Candy asked. "Has Richard said anything?"

"No," Lilith replied, "but it's not supposed to be one of their own, so it would probably be someone from the Montros family."

"That was his mother's house..."

"Obviously," Lilith said. "Montros and Augustus have been allies for generations, just like the Tagus and Groen families. That's what makes Veber's vote so important."

"Must be brilliant to be *her*," Candy said, referring to Lady Veber.

"Personally, I don't see why Richard can't nominate himself," Lilith said.

"It's tradition, dear."

Lilith rolled her eyes. "I don't give a damn about that."

"Lilith!" Candy admonished her.

"Well, I don't," she replied. "I'm having a son who could be heir to the throne if Richard only shared my vision."

"It sounds like you want an Augustus dynasty."

"Why not? We'd be better rulers than the other families. Richard's father proved that!"

"I suppose," Candy replied doubtfully. "But I don't see how you'll get the other families to go along."

Lilith stared at her untouched eggs.

"We'll see," she said.

As a robot, Burkebot was physically nothing like his namesake. Personality-wise, he was also unlike the late Lieutenant Burke, which Lord Rupert Tagus III reiterated on a regular basis.

"He's not half the man Lieutenant Burke was," Tagus said with the robot standing directly behind him.

"To be fair," Lady Veber said from across the table, "he *is* a robot."

Rolling his eyes, Tagus surveyed the Grove restaurant before uttering a dissatisfied grunt.

"I don't see why we had to meet here," he complained.

Lady Veber, wearing a turquoise pantsuit and a tiny blue hat pinned to her hair bun, stared back.

"I think we both know why I chose a public meeting," she replied.

Tagus clenched his teeth. "Because you *killed* my father."

"Because your *father* killed my *son!*" Lady Veber said, matching his angry gaze.

Dressed in a tunic bearing his family's colors, Tagus softened his expression and waved a hand in the air.

"Casualties of war," he said.

Burkebot watched attentively. These interactions between humans were always interesting, if not entirely logical at times. As the robot understood it, Tagus' father had killed Lady Veber's son in retaliation for her support of Hector Augustus' ascension to the throne. For her own part, Lady Veber killed the senior Tagus in revenge for the loss of her son. That much was clear. What baffled Burkebot was finding Tagus and Veber now sharing a table for brunch.

Fleshlings are endlessly confusing, the robot thought.

"Look at these people," Tagus said, referring to the other patrons. "Eating brunch like imbeciles. The very idea of brunch is ridiculous!"

"Is it?" Lady Veber replied, somewhat amused.

"Half measures," Tagus continued. "It should be either breakfast or lunch, not *both*!"

"Good point," she said without enthusiasm, "but perhaps we should discuss why you've asked to see me?"

"Yes, of course," Tagus replied. "I assume you can guess?"

"The conclave?"

"Obviously."

"It will be held on my family's planet, Lokeren, as always," Lady Veber said. "As is the tradition."

"And as is also tradition," Tagus replied, "House Veber will cast the deciding vote on who will become the next emperor."

"More than likely," she replied.

Tagus leaned closer, the sharp features of his face hanging over the table like a knife.

"Who will *you* vote for?" he asked.

Lady Veber became coy.

"How should I know?" she replied with a slow shrug. "The candidates haven't even been chosen yet."

"But you can guess," Tagus said.

"Well, the Augustus family cannot nominate someone from their house, so there could be candidates from House Montros, Groen, and Tagus. And mine of course."

"The Augustus family will vote for their ally, the Montroses, and the Groens will vote for me as head of the Tagus family."

Lady Veber nodded. "If all goes as it usually does."

"And you will act as king maker," Tagus replied.

"As it usually goes..."

Tagus reclined back in his chair, presumably to appear less threatening, Burkebot thought.

"I want you to consider voting for me," Tagus said, making his best attempt at a smile.

Lady Veber scoffed. "Why would I do that?"

"I realize you may fear retaliation if I were to become emperor," Tagus said.

"You'd imprison me on your coronation day," she replied.

Tagus shook his head. "Not necessarily."

"Have me executed then?"

"Not at all," Tagus said. "What if I signed a decree pardoning you of all responsibility for my father's death?"

Lady Veber was silent.

"In fact," Tagus went on, "I could do a great deal for you and your family. Your house has been king makers, true, but not much else. What if I could offer you more power and prestige than you could imagine?"

"Why should I trust you?" Lady Veber asked.

Tagus' smile curled at the edges.

"My father could have been emperor, but failed," Tagus said. "I'll do whatever it takes to make sure I don't follow in his footsteps."

It was big. A lot bigger than Henry Riff had expected.

When Thomas Martel had arrived at the Maycare estate, Benson the butlerbot had insisted that the detective relinquish his sidearm. Martel pulled Maxwell from his holster and handed it to the robot. Beside him, Henry thought he heard Jessica Doric gasp, but that might have been his imagination.

"I'm going to need that back," the detective said.

"I'll return it when you leave," Benson replied.

Lord Devlin Maycare, fashionably late as always, appeared in the atrium with his usual gusto.

"Detective Martel!" he shouted much more loudly than necessary, making Henry jump. "How the hell are you?"

"Good, Lord Maycare," the detective replied as they shook hands.

"Call me Devlin," Maycare replied. "How about we retire to my study?" Noticing Jessica, he said, "Jess, why don't you join us?"

Jessica, in a white blouse and tweed skirt, glanced at her assistant.

"What about Henry?" she asked.

Maycare's eyes widened. "Oh, I didn't see him there! Sure, he can tag along..."

Henry, both irritated at the slight yet thankful to be included, trailed behind the others. The study contained a fireplace and green leather chairs, along with a couch in front of the fire. The fire itself was not real, merely a holographic projection, but emitters behind it still radiated a comfortable warmth into the room.

Henry and Doric took the chairs on either side of the couch where Martel and Maycare sat down.

"I'll bring some refreshments," Benson said before disappearing through a side door leading to the kitchen.

Sizing up the detective, Maycare smiled and said, "Glad you could come on such short notice!"

"No trouble," Martel replied. "I rarely turn down a job or a free meal."

"I envy you," Maycare remarked. "The life of a private dick must be exciting!"

Henry noticed Martel's mouth form a wry grin.

"Well," the detective said, "it seems like your life can be pretty dangerous at times."

Maycare laughed. "That's true. In fact, that's why I've called you here."

Martel retrieved a datapad from his jacket. "Something about one of your races?"

"My racing sled exploded," Maycare replied, nodding emphatically. "And it was sabotage, plain and simple."

"Is there anyone who might want you dead?" the detective asked.

Personally, Henry could think of several people. Lord Maycare's former lovers and their husbands would make an impressive list...

"Not a one," Maycare replied. "I'm loved by just about everybody!"

"Then," the detective went on, "is there anyone who would benefit from you losing the race?"

"Well, I spoke to one fellow, Lord Grayson," Maycare said, "but he gave me his word as a gentleman he was innocent."

Martel raised an eyebrow. "That doesn't exactly *exclude* him, does it?"

"Of course it does!" Maycare replied with some outrage. "If a gentleman isn't as good as his word, what good is he?"

Martel said nothing but made a notation in his datapad. Meanwhile, Benson returned with a tray of cups, which he offered to each of them.

"TeeHee Tea," the robot said.

Taking a sip, Maycare nearly spat it out. "What flavor is this?"

"Pumpkin spice, sir."

"Why in heaven's name would you buy this?" Maycare asked incredulously.

"It was the request of Lady Candice," Benson replied.

Maycare cleared his throat.

"Alright then," he muttered under his breath, "carry on..."

Henry watched while Martel took a sip as well, but he didn't think the detective liked it either.

Just outside the city of Regalis, Ta Demona arrived at the door of a house resembling a traditional Japanese home. In her long, black robe, with a respirator covering most of her face, Demona was a frightening sight and her green skin didn't help. This had not always been the case. Before Kanet Solan recruited her for the Psi Lords, she had been a young priestess on the planet Technas Delphi, part of a monastic order called the Augmentor Sisterhood. Now, she was more machine than fleshling and a long way from the Temple on Technas Delphi.

She paused at the door, the paint on the wood flaked off in places. Raising her green knuckles, she knocked. After a few minutes, a woman opened the door. Demona saw a flash of recognition in the woman's mind and then nothing, as if a gate shut, blocking off her thoughts. This was not psionics, however. This woman had disciplined her mind in other ways.

"Hello, Lucy," Demona said.

Lefty Lucy, standing in the doorway, replied only with an icy glare. They knew each other from Lucy's previous work with the Psi Lords, but Demona wouldn't say they were friends.

"I'm here to see Roland," Demona went on.

Lucy turned and led her into the dojo and through to a side room where Roland was practicing against a wooden post. With jabs and kicks, the young man struck the post repeatedly. He stopped when he saw the two women enter, but his eyes were focused on the Psi Lord.

"It's *you*," he said.

"Don't look so surprised," Demona replied.

The boy stammered and Demona sensed his embarrassment.

"I mean," he said, "I didn't expect to see you *here*."

"It would seem neither did your mother," Demona said, motioning toward Lucy who had maintained a steady scowl.

"Right," Roland replied. "I forgot the two of you had worked together."

"Only briefly," the Psi Lord said. "She was quite the chatterbox."

Lucy made a sudden movement toward her but stopped when Demona formed a sphere of purple vapor in the palm of her hand.

"Now, now," Demona said. "Don't be so hasty."

Lucy took a step back and folded her arms across her chest.

"What is that?" Roland asked, pointing at the floating orb in Demona's hand.

Demona closed her fingers, snuffing out the purple sphere.

"It's called Dark Psi," she explained. "Your mother was wise to control herself..."

Demona felt impatience swelling in Roland's mind.

"Why are you here?" he asked. "Do you have new information or not?"

"I do," Demona said.

"Well?"

"Sixteen years ago," she replied coolly, "two members of the Imperial Intelligence Service entered a penthouse on the planet Galanis. Their mission was to kill the man and woman, and their child, who lived in the apartment."

"My parents..." Roland said aloud. "What were their names?"

"They were Lord Robert and Lady Josephine Groen, and their little son Jack." Demona replied.

"Groen? As in the Groens of the Five Families?"

"That's right."

Roland turned to Lucy, the only mother he had ever known. "Did you know about this?"

Lucy shook her head, while never taking her eyes off the Psi Lord.

"No," Demona said, "I don't suppose she would have. I strongly suspect the man who killed your parents kept her in the dark."

"So, what happened?" Roland asked.

"Apparently the mission went sideways," Demona went on. "Although one agent killed your father, the other agent, apparently named Pitt, stopped short of killing you after he had killed your mother."

"Why?" Roland asked.

"That I don't know," Demona replied. "I guess you'd have to ask him."

"You said there were two agents..." Roland remarked.

"The man named Pitt killed the other agent," Demona said, "which is probably why Pitt had to go underground and change his name."

"Do you know what he changed it to?" Roland asked.

"I do indeed," she replied. "He's now known as *Magnus Black*."

Popular travel writer Nick Reeves once said, "The coldest winter I ever spent was a summer on Grarfell." Also called the *Gray Old Man*, Grarfell was the home planet of the Gordians and, like the Gordians themselves, was known for being inhospitable. In low-lying areas, clouds spat rain year-round, while higher elevations consisted of frozen tundra and deep snowpack. The surface was such a miserable experience that the Gordians had moved underground, carving enormous city-states out of the rock beneath the mountainous landscape above.

Magnus Black had arrived at one such city, landing his ship, the *Starling*, on a pad of flattened stone surrounded by low hills. While Magnus took the short walk between the warm interior of his cockpit and an elevator leading down, cold rain belted his stubbly face and closely shaved head. Only his long leather coat kept the rest of him dry before he could take shelter in the lift.

Inside, the controls consisted of two buttons, up and down, and Magnus chose the latter. The elevator then dropped like a rock, producing the odd feeling in Magnus' stomach as if a trap door had opened. Eventually, the plummeting sensation slowed until the lift came to a complete stop several hundred feet below the surface. When the doors slid apart, the cacophony of the city assaulted his ears. Called *Kurkslag*, it was one of many city-states on the planet, each a domain of its own, ruled by mayors who resembled warlords more than politicians.

Magnus wasn't expecting a welcoming committee and he didn't get one. At most, the locals greeted him with the word *Dûrndûran*, which his translator said meant both "hello" and "go have sex with yourself." The rest of the time, the Gordians ignored him as none of their business. Magnus used the opportunity to explore the city.

Kurkslag was a series of great halls decorated with geometrical forms and sharp, linear edges. To their credit, the Gordians were master builders and engineers. Even underground, the towering ceilings of each hall gave the feeling of space as if the city was much larger.

On the third day of his visit, Magnus found himself among a throng of Gordians and off-worlders. Everyone, including Magnus, was facing the front of the great hall where a Gordian was standing before a table on a raised platform of stone.

Magnus knew him as Hogug, the mayor of Kurkslag.

Like most Gordians, Mayor Hogug had a pig-like face with tusks and a snout. Instead of a business suit, he wore robes and a crown more befitting a king. His constituents, many of whom were also on his payroll, cheered the mayor as he raised a mug of fungus beer.

"Here's to another four years!" he shouted, toasting his own re-election. "May they be as lucrative as the last twenty-four!"

Magnus watched the mayor guzzle from the mug with great interest. Fungus beer was, in fact, the mainstay of Gordian life on Grarfell where breweries kept busy around the clock. Gordians, wherever they might be, rarely went more than 24 hours without drinking some.

Mayor Hogug was no different.

He tipped the mug until the last drop of beer had drained away. With a mighty belch, the mayor slammed it down on the table and took a seat, calling to a servant for his pipe.

As a powerful crime boss, Mayor Hogug had many enemies, many of whom wanted him dead. A lesser assassin might have attempted to poison Mayor Hogug's beer, knowing the Gordian's proclivity for drinking. However, the mayor had not reigned for over twenty-four years by being a fool. Every keg in his cellar was carefully tested before a drop of fungus beer met Hogug's lips. Taking the pipe from his servant, the mayor was equally confident that the tobacco had been carefully screened for toxins.

Mayor Hogug brought a light to the bowl of the pipe and gave the stem a good suck. Failing to ignite the tobacco, he gave it another try. Meanwhile in the crowd, Magnus had put his hand in his pocket and was carefully feeling for the rounded edges of a device the size of a key fob. Finding it, he lightly pressed a button on the mechanism.

Up on the platform in front of his constituents, Mayor Hogug was still unsuccessfully puffing on his pipe when the mini-missile inside the stem fired, the exhaust sending the tobacco in the bowl shooting into the air. The missile traveled down the stem in the other direction and into the mayor's mouth, blasting through the back of his head. The mayor dropped the pipe and fell against his chair, smoke drifting out of his open mouth while singed tobacco leaves fluttered down around his lifeless body.

The contract fulfilled, Magnus Black made this way back to the surface and left the way he came.

CHAPTER SEVEN

On most days, a martini was Lord Winsor Woodwick's favorite drink when he felt low. Today, however, the dry botanicals of vermouth had abandoned him like his no-good roommate, Lord Radford Groen. Sitting in an oversized armchair, Woodwick ruminated on his troubles even as he accepted tea from his niece, Lady Candice, who had paid him a visit.

"This will cheer you up," Candy said.

His walrus mustache nearly touching the dark liquid, Woodwick took a drink.

"I say, what is this?" he asked.

"Pumpkin spice, Uncle Winnie," she replied.

"Just what the doctor ordered," he said but thought, *if he wanted to kill me.*

"Do you know when Lord Groen will be back?" Candy asked. "We planned on going to Mudderfield Downs to bet on the horses..."

"I really have no idea, my dear. The man's gone off his nut, I'm afraid. I'm not sure I *want* him to return in his current state."

The door to the apartment buzzed.

"Would you mind?" Woodwick eyed his niece imploringly.

"Of course."

Candy checked the monitor on the back of the front door and found the face of a young man, no more than sixteen, looking back. She thumbed the button beneath the monitor. "Hello?"

"Hi," the boy said from the other side, "I was hoping to speak with Lord Groen?"

"I'm afraid he isn't in at the moment," Candy replied and saw the young man's expression drop.

"That's okay," he said sadly and turned to leave, but stopped when the door opened behind him.

"Perhaps there's something I could help you with?" Candy said in the doorway.

Woodwick, listening to the conversation, cringed at the thought of meeting a stranger, but his niece brought the boy into the living room anyway like a child with a stray kitten. Woodwick did his best to straighten himself in the chair.

"Who's this, then?" he asked.

"That's right," Candy replied. "I didn't ask your name."

"Well, I usually go by Roland," the young man said, "but apparently my real name is Jack Groen."

"*Apparently?*" Woodwick asked.

"I was adopted," Roland replied. "I didn't know who my real parents were until recently."

"Oh, dear!" Woodwick said, mustering up more energy than he had expected.

"I was hoping to talk with Lord Groen about them," Roland said.

"Why didn't you go to the Groen estate?" Candy asked.

"They refused to see me," the boy admitted. "I don't think they believed me, to be honest."

"How bloody beastly!" Woodwick remarked. "Typical Groens if you ask me..."

"Now, Uncle Winnie..."

Woodwick raised an eyebrow, remembering something. "Dear me, we've forgotten to introduce ourselves. I'm Lord Woodwick and this is Lady Candice."

With a short bow of his head, Roland replied, "Nice to meet you."

"Well, I'm afraid Lord Groen is far afield at the moment," Woodwick went on. "I dare say I don't know where the chap is presently."

"If you could tell his lordship I came by," Roland said, "I would really appreciate it."

"Yes, of course," Candy replied for her uncle. "It was a pleasure to meet you."

Roland smiled, his youthful face betraying a hint of worry. When she had closed the front door behind him, Candy turned to Woodwick.

"Quite handsome, don't you think?" she said.

Returning to his dour mood, Woodwick lay back in his chair.

"Don't start," he said with more bitterness than he intended. "You're a gold digger after all, not a cradle robber..."

Her mouth ajar, Candy glared at him. "Uncle Winnie!"

The Greenwood Country Club might not have served brunch as famous as the Grove at the Emissary Hotel, but what the club lacked in crêpes and croissants, it made up for with immaculate fairways, putting greens like smooth carpet, and a fully stocked beverage cart driven by a robot dressed as a young woman. It was the latter that caught Lord Radford Groen's eye as he stumbled out of the underbrush along the course. The robot, wearing pink shorts and a tightly fitting gold shirt, had just rolled up with her cart at the tenth hole tee. Three men greeted her and began ordering drinks almost immediately. One of the men, wearing a panama hat, was Eugene "Ducky" Davenport.

"Can you make a Manhattan?" Ducky asked the robot.

"Sure can!" she chirped.

Groen nearly tripped over a sand trap rake as he lurched toward the tee box. His hair, a tangled mess, hung around his face. His expensive clothes were torn in places.

"Ducky!" he rasped.

"Good lord!" Ducky replied, seeing the man approach. "Who the hell are you?"

"It's me, Radford..."

"Oh, my," Ducky said, grabbing Groen under the arm with one hand while accepting the cocktail with the other. "What's happened to you?"

Groen fell to one knee. "I need your help."

Ducky laughed before taking a drink.

"Well, of course," he said with a smile.

"I've been looking all over for you..." Groen said. "I need more petals."

Ducky removed his hat and shooed the other two men away, giving him and Groen some privacy.

"You haven't been abusing my little gift, have you?" Ducky asked. "They're more of an 'as needed' kind of chem. You shouldn't be taking them all the time."

Groen tried getting back to his feet, but failed, his knees digging into the soft grass.

"I couldn't stop," he said, staring down. "Now I need more."

"Well, I can't help you," Ducky replied.

Groen looked up, straining his neck. "Why not?"

"It just wouldn't be seemly," Ducky said. "I have a reputation to uphold, you know!"

"But I'm so tired," Groen replied. "I feel weak..."

"Have you tried a cold shower?" Ducky suggested. "That perks me right up!"

"I can barely stand."

"Well, you came all *this* way, didn't you? Get something to eat and -- I'm saying this as a friend -- take a shower. You positively *reek*!"

"Are you coming?" one of the other golfers called as they climbed into their cart.

"Listen, Radford," Ducky whispered while leaning down to him. "Nobody likes a man who can't *act* like one. If I had known you couldn't handle those Lotus petals, I never would've offered them. Now, get yourself cleaned up and don't bother me again with this business." Ducky tipped his hat and smiled. "Ta-ta!"

Ducky boarded the cart and they drove away, leaving Groen on his knees, feeling sick.

"Can I get you a cocktail?" the robot asked.

"No," Groen replied quietly.

"Alrighty then!" the robot said cheerfully and left in her own cart, the bottles of gin and other spirits inside rattling as the little transport disappeared around a hill.

Usually when Mister Munge tugged rudely on an arm there was blood spray and screaming, not a blinding flash and waking up to the smell of his own burning flesh. That detective had dragged him out of the alley and back to Griefer turf, and for that Munge would pay back the favor, but the scars along his face were a constant reminder that the Cyberpunks deserved payback as well.

Standing in Kid Vicious' office, Munge barely heard what his boss was saying.

"Are you listening?" Kid asked.

"Yes," Munge replied.

"Like I was saying," Kid continued, "who does Big G think he is, calling a summit between me and Gregor Ivanovich? Gang wars are bad for business? I'll tell you what's bad for business: *Gregor Ivanovich!* The sooner he's dead the better!"

"Munge kill him," Munge said.

Kid cringed while looking at his enforcer. Munge had never been a natural beauty, but his new disfigurements made him a gruesome sight.

"No," Kid replied, glancing away, "I've got somebody else in mind..."

The speaker on Kid's desk buzzed and one of his men said, "That guy you sent for is here."

"Send him up," Kid replied.

Munge listened for the usual footsteps on the stairs outside, but not a sound came through the door until a man, like a dark ghost, pushed it open. His head and face were shaved to a fine stubble and he wore a black leather coat that reached the floor. His sharp, gray eyes surveyed the room and everyone in it the moment he walked in.

"Magnus Black," Kid said, "I've heard a lot about you..."

"I got your message," Magnus replied.

"I've got a job for you--"

"Who's this?" Magnus interrupted, gesturing toward the enforcer.

"This is my associate Mister Munge," Kid said.

"He looks like somebody used a cheese grater on his face," Magnus said.

Munge growled and took a step forward, but some primal instinct stopped him.

"Good boy," Magnus said before turning his attention to Kid. "What's the job?"

"The head of the Si-Sawat, Big G, has called a summit between me and my rival Gregor Ivanovich," Kid said. "Gregor and I have been at each other's throats and Big G thinks he can make peace between us."

"You disagree?" Magnus asked.

"Big G only cares about himself," Kid replied. "Apparently our gang war has scared away the high rollers from his casino so now he's acting all diplomatic like." Kid held out his arms, imitating Big G's girth. "Look at me, I'm a peacemaker!"

Munge chuckled, but the man in black remained stone-faced.

"Anyway," Kid went on, "I want you to come to the summit with me."

"And do what exactly?" Magnus asked.

"Kill Gregor Ivanovich, obviously!" Kid replied.

"Not exactly subtle," the assassin remarked.

"That's the point!" Kid shouted. "I want to get rid of Gregor and send Big G a message that he's not as big as he thinks he is. Kill two birds with one stone so to speak..."

"Alright," Magnus said. "I'll do it, but I want to get paid in advance."

Kid removed a credit stick from a drawer and slid it across the desk. "Yeah, I figured as much."

Magnus took the stick and dropped it into his pocket. "When's the summit?" he asked.

"In a few days," Kid replied. "And wear something nice. We've got *standards* to uphold."

Lord Radford Groen gathered the remainder of his energy and took a gravtaxi to Ashetown. This was not his first time in the district. Groen often visited the Fat Cat Casino, gambling away his family's fortunes at the craps table or roulette. Groen had never noticed all the garbage on the sidewalks before, but even in the darkness beneath a broken streetlamp, he saw the cracked concrete and abandoned vehicles parked along the curb. Still, even as a fog clouded his mind, Groen knew that Ashetown was the place to find chems.

Groen's datapad vibrated in his pocket. Pulling it out, he stared into the face of his roommate.

"Dear *lord*, Radford!" Lord Winsor Woodwick shouted. "You're positively a mess!"

"Piss off, Winnie..." Radford grumbled, but batted his disheveled hair down all the same.

"I say, that's a fine way to talk," Woodwick replied.

"I'm busy."

"Too busy for my niece?" Woodwick went on. "She was here earlier. Apparently the two of you were going to the track again, not that *I* was invited..."

Groen wiped his mouth with his sleeve.

"She doesn't need me," he said. "I taught her all I know about betting on the horses."

"Well, that can't have taken long," Woodwick replied. "Where in heaven's name are you?"

"Ashetown."

"At the casino?"

Groen hesitated. "No."

"You're looking for more of that chem, aren't you?" Woodwick asked accusingly. "Ducky called and said you made a scene at the country club."

"Ducky can go to hell."

Woodwick's walrus mustache rustled like a bush full of birds. "I say, Radford, this has gone too far!"

"You can go to hell too," Groen replied.

"If that's the case," Woodwick replied, "then I don't want you to come home, at least not until you've shaken this demon that's gotten hold of you."

Groen mumbled something unintelligible.

"One other thing," Woodwick said. "I don't know why I should bother, but a young man came to visit. He said he was a relative."

"Who?"

"Roland, I believe," Woodwick replied.

"Never heard of him," Groen said.

"Oh, he used another name too. *Jack,* I think."

"Jack?"

"Yes, Jack Groen," Woodwick replied.

Groen stopped on the broken sidewalk.

"That's impossible," he said. "How old was he again?"

"How should I know, Radford?" Woodwick protested. "In his teens, I suppose."

"I don't believe it."

"Really, Radford, I have no reason to lie. Honestly, I think I've had enough."

The screen went blank and Groen was alone again, or so he thought. From the shadows cast by the neon sign of a laundromat, the form of a man emerged. Lanky and with bad posture, he stepped out of the shadows. With an Irish accent, he said, "Evenin', sir, souns like ya in a bit of botha?"

"Who are you?" Groen asked.

"A friend, sir," man replied. "You lookin' for some petals then?"

"How did you know that?"

The man gave a knowing smile. "I've a keen eye for it. Lotus Eaters have the *look,* ya see."

"You can get me more petals?" Groen asked, a hint of desperation in his voice.

"Aye, I can," the man replied and beckoned Groen toward the door of the laundromat. While every fiber of his body told him not to, Groen followed. Once inside, the door closed behind him.

With a new case and an advance payment from Lord Maycare in hand, Thomas Martel decided to drop by the Sous-Sol for a drink. The stairway from the street down to the bar was even more dark and grimy than he remembered it, though it had only been a few days. Getting a taste of the high life in the West End may have colored his judgment, Martel concluded as he went inside.

"Louis wants to see you!" Red the bartender shouted, his only greeting.

Of course he does, Martel thought.

He wondered what strange outfit Louis Rion would be wearing this time, but Martel had to admit seeing a little brown dog in the office was the last thing he expected. At Louis' feet, a wire-haired dachshund watched Martel closely as the detective entered. Louis himself wore an overcoat with leather gloves and a tweed Trilby hat. To complete the ensemble, a dark mustache was glued above his lip.

"Bonjour, Monsieur Martel," he said, his faux accent more exaggerated than ever. "Merci beaucoup for yeuwr help with zat swine Monsieur Meung."

"Who?" Martel asked, barely understanding.

"Meung," Louis replied again.

"What?"

Louis grew irritated. "Meu-ng...Meu-ng!"

"Oh, *Munge*," Martel said.

"Of course!" Louis replied, whispering beneath his breath, "Idiot..."

"Actually," Martel said, ignoring the remark, "I just got a new case and could have paid my tab without running your little errand."

"C'est la vie," Louis replied. "Yeuw may drink freely again at Le Sous-Sol."

"Good to know," the detective said.

Martel eyed the dachshund. "Does your dog bite?"

"Non," Louis replied absentmindedly, his attention focused on a datapad on his desk.

The detective bent to pet the dog, but the dachshund leaped at him, biting Martel on the hand. Drawing back, he scowled at the bar owner.

"I thought you said your dog doesn't *bite*?" Martel asked.

Louis glanced at the animal. "Zat is *not* my dog."

Martel closed the office door behind him, his eye twitching, and sat on a stool at the bar.

"Whiskey!" he said.

Red poured the drink and pushed it in front of him. The bartender grinned, amused by Martel's mood.

"You think you've got it bad?" Red asked. "Try having him as a boss..."

Behind the bartender were pictures of his days as a boxer. As far as Martel knew, Red hadn't been particularly good at it and was deaf in one ear for his troubles.

"Do you ever miss boxing?" Martel asked.

Red scoffed. "Hell no!"

"I'm working a case that might have something to do with gambling," the detective remarked.

"Yeah?"

"Somebody sabotaged my client's racing sled," Martel went on. "Maybe to win a bet."

"Gambling's a dirty game," Red replied. "It wouldn't surprise me..."

"Boxing isn't exactly a clean sport either," Martel said. "You ever throw a fight?"

The bartender's eyes narrowed and he pointed a stubby finger at one of the scars on his wide forehead.

"You see this?" he asked. "I got this for *not* taking a dive!"

"Sorry."

"Whatever," Red replied, waving his hand.

"Can you think of anybody who might know if a fix was in?" Martel asked.

Red thought a moment and then replied, "Go see the Irishman."

Shady O'Shea, as he was called, worked the streets of Ashetown like the dealer in a game of Three-card Monte: just when you thought he was in one spot, Shady would turn up somewhere else. A jack of all trades, he could also get things done, usually under the table, and he did odd jobs for many of the gangs of Regalis.

It took a while for Thomas Martel to find him. As was often the case with underworld figures, Shady found you, not the other way around. After Martel had begun asking for him, Shady stepped out of an alley just as the detective was headed back to the Sous-Sol.

"You ben lookin' for me have ya?" Shady asked.

Martel nearly pulled Maxwell from his holster but stopped short after seeing Shady slumping in the shadows. Having known him since Martel was in the Regalis PD, he knew Shady was slippery but not dangerous.

"Yeah," Martel replied.

"Ha-ware-ya then, Shamus?" Shady went on. "Ben a whoil hasn't it?"

"I'm all right," the detective said. "I've been working a case..."

"So I've 'eard"

"Really?"

"Aye," Shady said. "For Lord Maycare no less."

"How did you know that?" Martel asked.

The Irishman smiled. "I've got ears haven't I?"

"Big ones apparently."

Shady pulled on the lobe of his right ear, perhaps checking for its size.

"Anyway," Martel continued, "that's why I wanted to talk to you."

Shady shook his head.

"Talk ain't cheap, innit!" he replied.

Martel grimaced, but pulled a credit stick from his pocket and handed the thumb-sized device to Shady who tucked it into a pocket of his own.

"Ah, to business then..." Shady said.

"Somebody sabotaged Lord Maycare's racing sled," Martel explained. "I think it's got something to do with illegal gambling."

"Why do ya s'pose it's *illegal* gamblin'?"

"Nobody made a sizable bet on Maycare losing or the racer who won," Martel replied. "If I'm right, it would have to be a bet placed under the table."

"Well, I wouldn't know about dat," Shady said, "but ya should talk to Jollux, I wager."

"You mean Gelatinous Bob, the loan shark?" Martel asked, using Jollux' nickname.

Shady waved his hands. "Aye, but I wouldn't be callin' 'im dat to his face. Killed a lad last week who done dat."

"What would a loan shark know about illegal gambling?"

"Are ya daft?" Shady replied. "Who do ya tink bankrolls 'alf the stakes in Ashetown, eh? I've ben doin' odd jobs for 'im as of late an' I can tell ya ol' Jollux is an even fatter cat than Big G."

"I always thought of him as a small timer," Martel remarked.

"He's ben movin' up in the world," Shady said.

Martel scratched his chin. "Seems like that's been happening a lot lately."

"Aye," Shady agreed, "but the bigger ya get, the bigger the target on ya back. Dat's why I stay skinny as a rail..."

Martel nodded grimly and wondered if he should go on a diet himself.

Ta Demona did not relish her visits to the Lotus dens. The leader of the Cyberpunks, Gregor Ivanovich, had made a deal with the Psi Lords, giving them full access to the minds of the unfortunates who slept away their lives in the dens under the influence of Lotus. In return, the Psi Lords gave Gregor's gang the most high-tech augmentations available. While a fair deal in principle, as far as Demona was concerned, she had not found a single mind with information that could prove useful.

Mostly, she thought it was a waste of time.

The smell of detergent and the solvents used to clean delicate fabrics filtered through her respirator as Demona entered the laundromat before walking into the flophouse in back. In the Lotus den itself, the air was cold and moist like a crypt. Silent too, except for the chorus of snoring that rose and fell from the Lotus Eaters.

One of the Cyberpunk thugs nodded at her but said nothing. His mind, which Demona had read many times before, was nothing but rage and stupidity. She doubted he had composed a single interesting thought in his life.

Demona passed along the corridor flanked by doorways on either side. She had no need to open the doors since the minds of those inside, amid their swirling dreams, were already accessible. Many of the dreamers, like the guard in front, were regulars at the den. They offered little in the way of lucrative intelligence. Most were destitute junkies living the last days of their miserable lives, an ending that Demona considered merciful if not long overdue. Yet her boss, Kanet Solan, sent Demona back to this place time and time again. It was a pointless fishing expedition and nothing more.

Quite by surprise, Demona felt something different behind one of the doors. Unlike the dregs of Ashetown, this mind was as new as it was educated. She stopped, shutting out the other thoughts until she focused entirely on this single consciousness. Peering into the man's dream, Demona felt this was more than mere fantasy. These were real memories mixed with the unreal.

The man was dreaming of a room in a luxury apartment with windows overlooking a city of skyscrapers. Handsome, he wore the green tunic of the Groen family. Delving deeper into the man's mind, Demona found his name: Lord Radford Groen.

A woman entered holding something bundled in a blanket.

"Josephine," Groen said. "Let me take a look at him..."

The woman let the blanket fall open, revealing the chubby face of a baby.

"We've named him Jack," she said proudly. "Isn't he beautiful?"

"Well, he has your eyes certainly," Groen said. "I don't recognize much else, I must say."

Josephine frowned. "Don't be silly."

"Curious, isn't it?" someone said.

Both Groen and Josephine turned their heads to see another man dressed in green. Through Groen's thoughts, Demona identified him as Lord Robert Groen, Josephine's husband and Groen's cousin. A few years older than Groen, Robert was taller with a warmer complexion and wide shoulders. He smiled, his eyes fixed on the baby, but his dark eyes were cruel.

"What's that?" Groen asked.

"It just seems strange," Robert went on, "that my son looks nothing like me..."

"I was just joking," Groen replied.

"I'm not," Robert said coldly.

Josephine's cheeks flushed. "What are you implying?"

"The two of you have always been close," Robert replied, "even before we were married."

"Come off it, Rob!" Groen protested. "Josie and I have never been more than friends."

"I'm not so sure..." Robert said.

"You're a fool!" Groen shouted, his own face reddening.

Behind them, the wall of the apartment melted and another man, like a specter emerging from the darkness, appeared. Older than the rest by at least thirty years, he commanded a sense of respect, even fear.

When Demona saw his face, she recognized him immediately.

"You're *both* fools!" he sneered.

CHAPTER EIGHT

As was the tradition, the Imperial Conclave would take place on the planet Lokeren, a world of island chains and vast, tropical oceans owned exclusively by the Veber family. Of the many estates dotting these islands, Lady Veber's favorite was a palace in the southern hemisphere. It had cube-shaped buildings painted white with domes of light blue, overlooking cliffs leading down to a beach of white sand and turquoise water.

Thoughts of the conclave far from her mind, Lady Veber lay on a towel spread over the hot sand. A large umbrella, decorated with a shell motif, provided much needed shade from the sunlight beating down. She was vaguely aware of her husband lying somewhere behind her, but most of Lady Veber's attention was focused on a young boy in the water, her son Philip.

After countless tries, Lady Veber had finally born a child, the spitting image of his father. The two of them were the only men in her life that she cared about, and spending these afternoons together were the happiest days of her life.

Philip played in the gentle surf. No more than ten, he splashed among the waves rippling into shore, his skin tanned to a light bronze.

"Look at me, Mommy!" he shouted.

Lady Veber smiled, shading her eyes. "Don't go out too far!"

"I won't!"

Lady Veber loved the sea. It had always welcomed her like a mother's embrace, but she had become wary of the ocean, knowing it could be deep and dangerous.

She turned to check on her husband, but he wasn't there. Lady Veber called his name but no one replied.

Then, like a memory lost in the sand, she remembered that her husband had died, killed when his gravcar crashed into the sea. She had worn black for a year, mourning his death.

The white sands of the beach turned dark as clouds covered the sun.

Philip's voice called out to Lady Veber. She looked back toward the sea, only to notice that her son was more distant now, his little arms waving just above the water.

Lady Veber struggled to her feet, the towel tangling between her legs. She ran to the edge where the sea met the shore.

"Philip!" she shouted.

She saw him yelling but the sound refused to reach her. His lips moved, but she couldn't hear what he was saying. She took a step toward the water but, looking down, the turquoise had turned black and opaque. In just a few inches of water, Lady Veber could no longer see her feet.

"Philip!" she cried again, but the boy was no longer visible. Was he too far out or had the ocean dragged him down?

He was gone.

"Philip!"

One of her handmaidens was at her side. "Wake up! Wake up!"

Opening her eyes, Lady Veber lay in her bed, not on a beach.

"You were having a nightmare," the handmaiden said.

Lady Veber coughed and held a hand against her hot cheek, even as the memory of the dream faded rapidly from her mind.

"I'm all right," she said, waving off the servant. "I'll be fine..."

The handmaiden bowed and left the bedroom while Lady Veber sat up. This was the estate in the southern hemisphere of her family's planet, Lokeren. It had always been her favorite with its white beaches and turquoise sea. It was also the place where her son Philip had died, poisoned by Lord Tagus' father. Tagus would arrive soon, along with the other representatives of the Five Families.

She had to prepare for their arrival and the beginning of the conclave.

In the evening, Gregor Ivanovich and his bodyguard arrived at the Fat Cat Hotel to attend the summit between the Cyberpunks and the Griefers. A valet opened the gravcar door beneath the crystal chandeliers of the porte-cochère at the main entrance of the hotel. The bodyguard, named Ward, stepped out of the car first, followed by his boss who seemed unimpressed by the opulence.

"Cheap glass," Gregor remarked, motioning toward the chandeliers.

"Sure, boss," Ward replied.

While most of the other Cyberpunks had augmented their bodies with electronic devices and weaponry, Ward had chosen hair implants instead. This meant he was not as heavily armed as his comrades, but he had the most elaborate coiffure of anyone in the gang. His boss might have scoffed at chintzy decor, but Ward wondered if he could steal a chandelier and hang it in his one-bedroom apartment.

The manager of the hotel, a Tikarin with black and brown fur, greeted them in the lobby before politely, if not gently, patting them down for weapons. After removing several handguns and Gregor's sword, the manager directed them to a private elevator, which took them to Big G's penthouse. Big G himself met them when the lift doors opened, his head dwarfed by the orange fluff of his colossal belly.

He waddled closer.

"Hello, boys!" Big G shouted, spreading his stubby arms. "Welcome to my hotel!"

Past the Tikarin's stomach, Ward spotted Kid Vicious in a sunken living room, sitting beside an unusually tall man with horrific burns across half his face.

"It's about time you got here, Gregor!" Kid yelled.

"Now, now," Big G said. "Let's remain cordial. After all, you're here under my protection. Consider yourself as safe here as at your mamma's *teat*."

Gregor grimaced at the thought. "That remains to be seen."

"Did they check him for weapons?" Kid asked.

"Of course," Big G replied. "Everybody's been searched thoroughly."

He beckoned Gregor and his bodyguard to follow and led them down into the sunken recess.

"I didn't know that monster was going to be here," Gregor said, eyeing Munge.

"Have some respect!" Kid replied angrily. "Munge is my best man."

"Well, *your* best man killed *my* best man," Gregor said.

Kid snickered. "I guess that shows whose man was *really* best, doesn't it?"

Gregor, who had just sat, jumped up again but Big G hissed, causing the Cyberpunk boss to stop.

The orange feline wiped some spittle from the side of his mouth.

"You will both behave while you're under my roof," he said sternly. "You guys may be unarmed but my men are not, so don't make any trouble, understand?"

Gregor and Kid Vicious nodded.

"That's better," Big G said, his expression changing to a smile. "Now, we've assigned each of you a suite. Go and relax tonight and we'll get to business in the morning."

The two warring sides stood together, but wisely took the elevator separately. Ward was especially eager to see what the suite had to offer, wondering if there was a hairdryer and luxury haircare products.

While Lady Veber waited at the transmat platform overlooking the cliffs near her estate on Lokeren, the ocean breeze played with the edges of her taffeta dress. With two of her servants beside her, Lady Veber watched as a pair of forms slowly materialized. She had little trouble recognizing the first one, his angular shoulders and arrogant posture identifying him as Lord Rupert Tagus III. The other shape was a bit rounder in the face and more relaxed in demeanor. As his features grew into focus, a hint of scruff became visible around his chin, and a thin mustache beneath his nose.

Lord Vincent Groen, Lady Veber thought.

The transmat process complete, both men stepped down from the platform and gave their host the briefest of greetings.

"Lady Veber," Vincent said, "so nice to see you again."

"The pleasure's mine," she replied.

"Is Richard here yet?" Tagus asked gruffly.

"He's due shortly," Lady Veber said.

"I hope they won't be staying near us," Tagus went on.

"Not at all," she replied with a curt smile. "You all have your own wings, I assure you."

Apparently satisfied, Tagus grunted and gave Lord Groen a nod. "Let's get inside. This wind is blowing sand in my eyes."

"I hope I can get the market reports on this planet," Vincent remarked while one of Lady Veber's servants led them away.

Their voices trailed off, lost in the whispering breeze. Lady Veber took a deep breath, drawing the salty air into her lungs. She wondered what kind of sounds Tagus would make if she shoved him off the cliff. The beach at the bottom would certainly make it easy to bury his body.

She stopped herself.

Killing one of his family was enough. At least for now...

The air crackled and another shape began to form on the transmat pad. This time, the outline was singular in its femininity, with graceful curves like the petals of a flower. When complete, Lady Olivia Montros stood on the platform in a pale rose-colored dress. Blessed with high, angelic cheekbones, but cynical eyes and a sarcastic smile, she grinned at seeing Lady Veber.

"Rebecca," Olivia said. "You haven't aged a bit!"

This, Lady Veber knew, was the exact opposite of what Olivia intended to convey.

"Good to see you too," she replied.

"We missed you at the Imperial ball," Olivia continued, casting a glance at the cloudless sky above the turquoise waters below. "But if I owned a planet like this, I wouldn't want to leave either!"

Olivia came down the stairs and the two women exchanged kisses on their cheeks.

"Tagus and Groen have arrived already," Lady Veber said. "Prince Richard will be here momentarily."

"Well, I won't wait for him," Olivia replied. "I need to freshen up a bit."

Lady Veber motioned to her servant who took her to the main building. Alone, Lady Veber had only the final guest to arrive and within a few minutes, the air thickened into another human form.

"Prince Richard," she said. "Welcome to Lokeren."

Dressed in his official garb, the red and gold of the Augustus family, the prince acknowledged her with a magnanimous wave of his hand.

Pompous ass, Lady Veber thought.

On one of the upper floors of the Fat Cat Hotel, a waiter pushed a hovercart with a food tray to the door of Gregor's suite. Dressed in a red vest with a white apron tied around his waist, the waiter knocked. Within moments, a bodyguard with rich, flowing hair swung open the door.

"What's this?" he asked.

"Courtesy of Big G," the waiter replied.

"All right, bring it in."

The waiter pushed the cart into the suite, but the bodyguard stopped him from going farther.

"I need to search you," he said.

The waiter raised his arms above his head while the gangster patted him down. Unlike the bodyguard, the waiter's head was shaved.

Apparently convinced the waiter was unarmed, the bodyguard pointed at the shiny dome at the center of the food tray. "What's under there?"

The waiter raised the dome, revealing a plate covered in potatoes and a steak.

"Filet mignon," the waiter said, setting the cover to the side.

The guard hesitated.

"Well, the boss is taking a shower," he said, "so I should probably taste this in case it's poisoned."

"Be my guest."

Taking a steak knife and a fork from the tray, the bodyguard cut into the juicy meat. He sampled the steak and set the utensils back on the tray.

"That's good," he mumbled, chewing loudly. "What's your name?"

"Magnus," the waiter replied.

"You worked here long?"

"Not long," Magnus said.

Swallowing, the bodyguard turned toward the bedroom.

"I'll see if the boss is out of his shower..." he said.

In a smooth, fluid motion, Magnus Black removed the knife from the tray. With his left hand, he grabbed a handful of the bodyguard's luscious hair, using it to yank the gangster's head back to expose his neck. With a quick stroke, Magnus slit the man's throat, painting the opposite wall with blood.

The bodyguard fell lifeless to the carpet, now soaked in a puddle of dark red.

Magnus reached along the underside of the cart and pulled out a square device taped there. Little more than a small box with a button on top and a coil of wires in the front, it sat snugly in the palm of Magnus' left hand.

With the dripping knife in his other hand, Magnus moved quietly into the darkness of the bedroom, the only light coming from the bathroom doorway along with the sound of running water. Magnus held the device in front of him and, holding down the button, made sweeping motions back and forth until he heard a pained shout come from the bathroom. Magnus released the button, letting the device drop to the floor.

"Ward!" a man's voice shouted. "Ward!"

The running water stopped abruptly and a man, dressed in a robe, appeared in the doorway with a small pistol.

"Lights on," Gregor Ivanovich said.

The bedroom lights came up immediately and Gregor pointed the gun at Magnus in the center of the room. The gang boss touched the smoldering hole that had once been his augmented eye.

"What the hell did you do?" he demanded.

"I used an electromagnetic pulse to short out your eye so you couldn't see through the walls," Magnus replied coldly. "I guess I wasn't expecting you to be armed..."

"A snub pistol can't shoot far, but it's easy to miss during a pat down," Gregor said. "Did you say EMP? What kind?"

"Gamma ray."

"Are you crazy?" Gregor shouted. "That'll give me cancer!"

"You don't have that kind of time," Magnus said. "Lights out."

The bedroom lights went dark instantly. No longer able to see with his x-ray eye, Gregor failed to notice Magnus roll out of the way as the snub pistol fired, illuminating the room briefly with the flash. While the assassin had deftly moved from his previous position, Gregor had not, allowing Magnus to throw the steak knife accurately through the darkness, the blade lodging deeply into Gregor's skull.

The boss took a step backwards before falling through the doorway into the bathroom.

The day after the representatives from the Five Families had arrived on Lokeren, two of them were finishing breakfast. Lord Rupert Tagus III had just massacred a soft-boiled egg on toast while Lord Vincent Groen was watching an off-world sportscast on television. A commercial appeared on the screen:

WATCH THIS SUNDAY AS YOUR LOCAL
XENO LEAGUES PLAY BLOOD BALL!
NOW WITH TWICE AS MUCH BLOOD
AND THREE TIMES MORE BALLS!

"Turn that off!" Tagus demanded, wiping egg yolk from his mouth.

Vincent obliged and the monitor went blank.

"Not a sports fan, I take it?" Vincent asked.

"It's a waste of time," Tagus replied. "War is the only game worth playing."

After a pause, Vincent wondered aloud, "What do you think Olivia is having for breakfast?"

"If you're referring to Lady Montros," Tagus scoffed, "I assume she's having breakfast with Richard. Plotting her ascension to the throne no doubt!"

"You think Olivia will nominate herself?" Vincent asked.

"Of course."

"That would be something," Vincent remarked, "having her as Empress."

"Not if I can help it," Tagus replied.

"Well, you can count on me."

"I should hope so!" Tagus said. "And your family will be duly compensated as usual."

Vincent nodded. "My family appreciates it."

Tagus lifted a fork from the table for the sole purpose of pointing it accusingly at Lord Groen.

"You know I've been hearing stories about your uncle Radford," Tagus said. "You need to rein that man in!"

"Uncle Radford has always been a black sheep," Vincent said, "especially after my uncle Robert was murdered. He's never been the same since."

"Why not?"

"I don't know for sure," Vincent went on, "but he took my aunt and uncle's death quite hard."

Tagus rolled his eyes.

"Weakness," he said. "Pure and simple."

"I suppose so," Vincent replied. "We should get a move on. It's time..."

Lord Tagus and Groen found their way to the main dining hall where a round table, surrounded by five chairs, filled most of the room. Prince Richard and Lady Olivia Montros had already taken their seats while Lady Veber met the others as they entered through a pair of grand doors.

"Are we late?" Vincent asked.

"Not at all," Lady Veber replied.

"I'm sure the Prince doesn't mind waiting," Tagus said, giving Richard a vile grin.

"I can always wait for your inevitable defeat," the prince replied, which drew a laugh from Olivia.

"Alright," Lady Veber said impatiently. "Let's sit down and get this over with."

A servant pulled a chair out for Lady Veber beside Olivia, while Vincent and Tagus occupied the remaining two places. Tagus made a point of taking the chair beside Prince Richard, eager to show his lack of deference to the prince. Richard, for his part, ignored him and focused his attention on Lady Veber who was once again speaking.

"This opens the Imperial Conclave," she said, motioning to the others with a wave of her hands. Seeing little response, she continued. "In accordance with tradition, we will begin with a round of nominations and then, after however much deliberations are needed, we will commence with voting on those nominations."

Tagus stifled a yawn which brought a quick glare from Lady Veber.

"Let's get on with it, shall we?" he replied.

"Very well," she said. "I will start with Lady Montros and move around the table."

Olivia, her blond hair pulled back from her sharp, piercing eyes, smiled like a cat about to eat a mouse.

"On behalf of the Montros family," she said, "I nominate myself for the next Empress."

Although Lady Veber nodded, Tagus and Vincent showed little in the way of emotion while Prince Richard stared impatiently at the section of table directly in front him.

"Very good," Lady Veber said. "I will abstain from nominating anyone and pass the turn to Lord Groen."

To her left, Vincent bowed his head before turning his eyes to Lord Tagus.

"I nominate Lord Tagus," he said. "The next Emperor of the Imperium!"

Tagus made an effort to feign surprise, even if the nomination was a surprise to no one. His attempt at humility was even less convincing.

"Thank you very much, Lord Groen," Tagus said. "I accept your nomination and hope that the rest of you will see the rightfulness of my future reign. After my father was unjustly passed over the last time this conclave was held, it is only fitting that I, his son, be the next to wear the crown."

Vincent smiled, but the others failed to follow suit.

"Alright, Lord Tagus," Lady Veber began, "we will now recess while we discuss our votes..."

On the opposite side of the table, Prince Richard cleared his throat.

"Actually," he said, "I would like to speak, if you don't mind."

"It's not necessary for you to affirm Lady Montros' nomination," Lady Veber replied, her eyebrows raised in surprise.

"I don't intend to," he said. "I wish to nominate someone as well."

Olivia, her face contorted, leaned toward Prince Richard but he waved her away. The rest merely stared at the prince.

"As you wish," Lady Veber said.

Pushing out his chair, Prince Richard got to his feet so he stood taller than anyone else at the table.

"After much thought," he said, "I am nominating *myself*."

The suite for the Griefers was on a different floor than the Cyberpunks. Magnus Black entered without knocking, using the keycard Kid Vicious had given him earlier in the day.

Kid was waiting impatiently.

"Is it done?" he asked from across the room.

"It's done," Magnus replied.

Kid laughed, shaking his fist in the air. "Suck on that, Gregor!"

Unlike Gregor Ivanovich, the boss of the Griefers was dressed in his usual attire, jeans and a t-shirt, and not a bathrobe provided by the hotel. A complimentary bottle of Champagne sat empty in an ice bucket on a glass table just in front of where Kid was standing.

"Have you been celebrating early?" Magnus asked.

"Damn right!" Kid yelled, almost losing his footing. "Gregor was a pain in my ass and I'm glad the bastard's dead!"

After catching his breath, he went on, "Did he scream when he died?"

Magnus shook his head, showing the snub pistol he had retrieved from Gregor's body. "But he had this..."

Kid laughed again.

"We used to call those belly pistols," he said, "because you had to stick it in a guy's belly before pulling the trigger, or you'd miss."

"He apparently smuggled this one past security."

"Sneaky little shit," Kid remarked. "Gregor never liked playing by the rules... not that it did him any good in the end."

Magnus gave the room a quick glance. "Where's your burnt friend?"

"Munge?" Kid asked. "I sent him home. Big G's security is enough to keep me safe while I'm here."

"Good," Magnus replied and pointed the pistol at Kid.

"What's this?" the Griefer boss asked, the smile melting from his face.

"Gregor wasn't the only target tonight," Magnus replied.

"The hell?" Kid said. "I paid your contract!"

Magnus pulled a credit stick from the apron around his waist.

"I've been meaning to give this back," he said, tossing the tiny device across the room and onto the table. "It turns out somebody hired me *before* you did."

Kid sneered.

"Go ahead and shoot," he said. "Do you really think you can hit me from all the way over *there* with that pop gun?"

Magnus fired two shots, both striking Kid between the eyes. His mouth still frowning, the boss fell face-first onto the table, shattering the glass into jagged pieces.

"Yes," Magnus replied.

Magnus dropped the gun to the floor and left. Taking a private elevator, he arrived at the penthouse suite on the top floor. Big G stood in his sunken living room, rubbing his furry belly.

"Is it done?" he asked.

"It's done," Magnus said.

CHAPTER NINE

The information from Shady O'Shea led Thomas Martel to an old mansion in the Middleton district. A wall surrounded the property, but the detective could see the three-story home through the wrought-iron gate. Paint was peeling off the walls, but fresh scaffolding suggested somebody was renovating the place.

Martel rang the bell beside the gate.

"What do you want?" a gruff voice asked over the speaker.

"I'm Detective Thomas Martel. I'm here to ask Jollux a few questions."

"Bugger off!" the voice replied.

Martel turned to leave when a different voice spoke. "Alright, come on in."

A buzzer sounded and Martel heard the lock unlatch. Pushing on the cold iron, Martel walked through the now open gate. The path to the front door wound through tangled weeds and patches of dead grass. Even before Martel had set foot on the front step, the door opened and a man, dressed as a butler, stood in the entranceway. Martel noted that the man's clothes were tight around the arms and shoulders, concealing the muscles of a thug underneath.

Checking Martel for weapons, he removed Maxwell from its holster and put it aside on a table cluttered with several other guns of various types.

"This way," the servant said, his face bearing scars from what Martel assumed was a knife fight.

The inside of the house reflected the same dingy appearance as the exterior, although there was evidence of new wallpaper in places to cover the black mold growing on the walls. The servant took Martel through to a hothouse in the back, a glass enclosure where the temperature was stifling and the air hung with oppressive humidity. Martel removed his coat but felt a trickle of sweat already running down his back.

The hothouse was filled with orchids and exotic plants, their green leaves brushing against Martel's face as he walked past. In the center, on a wide bench of teak, a creature sat on spindly legs, tucked beneath a wide belly like a fat Buddha. A waddle dangled from a weak chin, hiding a near non-existent neck. The being's big yellow eyes surveyed Martel as he approached, and he stretched long, slender fingers in a beckoning gesture toward the detective.

"Thomas Martel, the private eye," Jollux said. "I've heard of you."

"I'm flattered," Martel replied, wiping sweat from his forehead. "Quite a place you have here."

"This? Oh, I *inherited* it from somebody who owed me money. It's a bit run down, but given time I expect it to regain some of its former glory."

"Do you always keep it so hot in here?" Martel asked.

"My apologies," Jollux replied. "It reminds me of my home planet, a jungle world, you know."

"Got it."

"Now," Jollux said, "what brings a PI to my doorstep?"

"I'm investigating a racing sled crash," Martel said. "Somebody tampered with the sled and I think it was to win a bet on the race."

"Oh, dear," Jollux replied, his eyes rolling in his head. "Who would go to such extremes?"

"I was hoping you could help me find out."

"Well, whose sled was it?"

"Lord Devlin Maycare's."

A chuckle came from deep inside the loan shark's stomach. "Oh, *him*. Yes, I remember hearing about the crash. Can't say I'm surprised though. He's a bit reckless, isn't he?"

"I looked at the sled," Martel replied. "It was definitely sabotaged."

"In that case," Jollux went on, "perhaps someone had a grudge?"

"I've looked into that too," Martel said. "Nobody appears likely."

Jollux waved his hand at the servant who still remained nearby. "Bring us some refreshments, won't you?"

"I'm fine," Martel said.

"Nonsense," Jollux replied dismissively. "It's no trouble."

"I'm told you front betting off the books," Martel said. "I was wondering if you recall any bets on that race, especially anybody betting on Lord Maycare to lose."

"I'm a legitimate banker, Mr. Martel," Jollux said. "It's true I loan money to those in need, especially those who the major banks refuse to serve. However, I would never dream of backing anything illegal."

"I'm not a cop," Martel replied. "I don't care if your business is legal or not."

Jollux smiled. "Perhaps, but loose lips sink ships, as they say..."

The servant brought a tray with two tall glasses of lemonade. Martel took one and drank a sip while the servant placed the tray and the other glass on a side table.

"Speaking of which," Jollux continued, "I'm curious who suggested I might have the answers you're seeking."

"Nobody," Martel said. "Gelatinous Bob is well known in Ashetown."

Jollux's big eyes narrowed.

"I detest that nickname," he said. "Fat shaming and such..."

"Sorry."

"Are you quite sure you won't tell me who sent you?" Jollux pressed. "I have a pretty good idea who it was. An Irishman perhaps?"

Martel, who was already sweating profusely, felt droplets collecting in his eyebrows. The room was also turning murky. He glanced at the glass in his hand.

"Are you alright, Mr. Martel?" Jollux asked.

The glass, slick with condensation, slipped between Martel's fingers. He took a step toward the exit, but his legs were weak and rubbery. The heat bore down on him like a heavy blanket.

The last thing Martel saw before passing out were the shoes of the thug masquerading as a butler. He noticed they were caked in a reddish mud, and then everything went black.

Jessica Doric and Henry Riff were examining one of the many artifacts displayed in Lord Maycare's hallways when the sound of a commotion echoed down the corridor. Following the noise, Doric and Henry ran through a doorway into the media room where a television monitor took up most of one wall. On the screen, the armored bodies of non-humans were throwing themselves at each other while another non-human was carrying an oblong-shaped ball. Their shouts and screams filled the room.

Also, the unexpected squawks of Lady Candice Groen.

Doric and Henry slid to a halt on the parquet floor, their eyes fixated on Candy and Lord Maycare sitting on a couch in front of the giant screen.

"What's going on in here?" Doric asked.

"It's called *Blood Ball*," Maycare replied. "Have you heard of it? Candy brought it to my attention--"

Candy, who held a pennant in one hand that read *Boneyard Bruisers*, clenched her perfect teeth as a Gordian on the monitor knocked another player off his feet.

"Yeah!" she shouted.

Doric, her eyes and mouth open, stared in horror and disbelief.

"You like this, Lady Candice?" she asked.

Barely able to look away, Candy replied, "Of course! It's great fun!"

The fun appeared to take place on a green field of grass with two lines of opponents, mostly Gordians and a few Draconians, each carrying tall, plastic shields. At the start of each play, a referee blew a whistle and the two phalanxes slammed together in a great clamor while, behind the offensive line, another non-human took the ball and tried running around the outside. A fast moving Tikarin met the ball runner, slamming him to the ground. He did not move, lying on the grass in a pile of arms and legs.

"See?" Candy shouted. "Great fun!"

"Why are they all non-humans?" Doric asked.

"Humans aren't allowed by law," Candy replied, "for their own protection."

Maycare spied Henry still in the doorway, his shoulders slouched and his hands covering his eyes.

"Oh, come on, Henry," Maycare said. "It's not that bad!"

"It frightens me," Henry whispered through his fingers.

"Well, it's called *Blood Ball* after all," Maycare replied.

"And you can bet on it too," Candy said. "There's even a dead pool!"

"This is terrible," Doric remarked, mostly to herself, but clearly audible to the others.

"Don't be silly," Candy said. "They're just xenos after all. And anyway, they deserve to have their own sports, don't they? Devlin's sports only allow humans."

"That's true," Maycare admitted sheepishly.

"And you bet on this?" Doric asked.

Candy hesitated.

"Sometimes," she said reluctantly. "Uncle Radford got me started."

"That figures," Maycare remarked. "How's he been doing?"

For the first time, Candy's eyes left the screen and stared at her lap. "We haven't heard from him in *days*!"

"What?" Doric asked.

"He called us from Ashetown," Candy went on, "but we haven't heard from him since."

Although Doric was not surprised to hear something terrible had happened to Lord Groen, she made an effort to be helpful. "Have you talked to the police?"

Candy scoffed. "They've been no help at all! I think they're *afraid* to go into Ashetown."

"I have a man," Maycare said, placing his hand on Candy's knee. "Maybe he could look into it for you..."

"The detective?" Henry asked.

"Martel," Maycare replied. "He'll know what to do!"

For countless years, the city of Regalis had dumped its trash in a corner of Ashetown called the Boneyards. Mounds of discarded machines and decommissioned robots became mountains of corroded parts and forgotten refuse. With every rain, the water filled with rust and seeped into the surrounding dirt, turning the ground into reddish mud.

When Thomas Martel opened his eyes, his face was planted neatly in the crimson clay, streaks of it in his hair and smeared across his face. His body hurt, especially his head which pounded like someone was striking him again and again with a ball peen hammer.

A few feet away, Maxwell's brushed chrome lay partially submerged in a puddle. Wearily, Martel got to his feet to retrieve the gun and only then noticed someone lying in the mud on the other side. From the clothes, he looked like Shady

O'Shea, although identification was difficult since the top of his head appeared to be gone.

Martel recognized the damage Maxwell could do.

Above a ridge of broken refrigerators, three gravcars bearing the insignia of the Regalis PD rose like the heads of a hydra with flashing red and blue lights. For a moment, Martel considered running, but there was really no point. The police would gladly have shot him before he went more than a few steps.

"Don't move!" a commanding voice said over a loudspeaker. "Stay where you are!"

Martel complied.

Several hours later, he was sitting with his hands shackled to a metal table in a windowless room while two homicide detectives paced back and forth. Martel knew their real names from when he was on the Force, but he preferred to call them *Wingus* and *Dingus*.

"Let's go over this again," Detective Dingus said.

"You don't know it by heart by now?" Martel asked.

Police protocol normally called for hitting the suspect with a phone book at this point, but since nobody used phone books anymore, Detective Wingus jabbed an electrical prod into Martel's stomach. The device had to be recharged after each interrogation, but it didn't leave a mark, so the result was the same. For his part, Martel felt every muscle in his body burn like they had set him on fire.

After his muscles unclenched, he scowled at his abuser.

"You must have a hell of an electricity bill," Martel said through gritted teeth.

Wingus snickered, pointing at the table where a clear evidence bag contained an unloaded Maxwell.

"That cannon there was fired twice, and you had gunpowder residue on your hands," he said. "We've got you dead to rights..."

"I don't suppose Gelatinous Bob vouched for me?" Martel asked.

"We talked to him," Dingus replied. "He said he never met you."

Damn good lemonade though, Martel thought.

"Now tell us why you killed O'Shea!" Wingus shouted, pounding on the table.

"How did you know I was there in the Boneyards?" Martel asked instead.

"Anonymous tip--" Wingus started before Dingus cut him off.

"Never mind that," Dingus said, "this has been a long time coming, Martel, ever since you cut out on your partner and the department."

Still muddy from lying in the dirt, Martel glared up at the homicide detective.

"From where I'm sitting," Martel said, "it's better to be knee deep in my own muck than whatever you two are swimming in."

Wingus gave the detective another jolt from the electric prod when the door opened and two men stood in the doorway. One was a lawyer type in a suit while the other was Lord Maycare.

"What the hell is this?" Dingus asked.

The lawyer shoved a datapad into his hands. "We have a court order for Mister Martel's immediate release on bail."

"We're not done with him yet!" Wingus protested.

"Yes, you are," Maycare said. "Now undo those handcuffs..."

Reluctantly, Dingus unlocked the shackles and Martel joined Maycare and the lawyer in the doorway.

"What about Maxwell?" Martel asked.

"I'm afraid that's still evidence," the lawyer said. "You can get it back after the trial."

Between the two sneering detectives, Maxwell sat alone in the evidence bag on the table. Martel gave the gun a final glance before leaving, nodding to the weapon as if to say, "I'll be seeing you soon."

In the Imperial palace, the television in the Emperor's private residence had such high resolution, Prince Richard could count the pores on Sylvia Flax's nose as she spoke.

"In a stunning development," she said on the screen, "VOX News has learned that Prince Richard has nominated himself at the Imperial Conclave. This unprecedented action has sent shock waves throughout the government. Meanwhile, Lady Veber has temporarily suspended the conclave while its members deliberate on what to do next..."

"Well," the Emperor remarked while giving his son the side eye, "you've really screwed it up this time."

Richard adjusted uncomfortably in his chair.

"I don't think so," the prince said after a pause.

"Lilith is responsible for this, isn't she?" the Emperor asked. "This has her fingerprints all over it."

"It was my decision, Father. I don't appreciate you dragging my wife into this conversation."

"Sounds like she dragged *you* into this conversation..."

"Lilith is at the hospital with contractions," Richard continued. "She could have the baby at any moment."

"Mazel tov!" the Emperor remarked. "A bit early though, isn't she?"

Richard tried his best not to scowl at his father. "Yes."

"Don't be cross, boy," the Emperor said. "Family comes before all this other nonsense..."

"Exactly!" Richard replied. "Why do you think I nominated myself? I wanted my son to be safe from people like Tagus!"

"Then why not support Olivia Montros?" the Emperor asked.

"You know her as well as any of us," Richard said. "Sometimes I think she'd be just as bad as Rupert."

"Careful," his father replied. "Your mother was a Montros. You're a product of both our houses, Augustus *and* Montros."

"But Olivia is *not* my mother and I don't trust her to run the Imperium as well as you or I."

"What makes you think you'd be a better emperor?"

"What do you think I've been doing for years now?" Richard replied. "Whenever you were loath to make decisions, I had to do it for you!"

The old man rose from his chair, his eyes trained on his son. "How dare you!"

"It's the truth," Richard replied coolly.

A tired sigh escaped from the Emperor's chest.

"Perhaps you're right," he said. "I may be guilty of coasting of late, but that doesn't mean you can throw tradition aside whenever it suits you. Withdraw your nomination before you destroy what we've been building here for centuries."

Richard stood and bowed his head to his father.

"I'll think about it," the prince replied.

"You do that," the Emperor said, putting a hand on Richard's shoulder. "In the meantime, go see your wife at the hospital. I was too busy being emperor to be there when *you* were born..."

Maycare's private gravcar dropped Martel at the corner of Marlowe and Vine. Although his shirt and pants were still splattered with mud, the detective went down to the Sous-Sol instead of up to his office. He decided that he needed a drink more badly than a fresh change of clothes.

"You look worse than usual," Red remarked, pouring a shot of whiskey at the bar.

"Thanks," Martel replied, taking a seat on the closest stool.

The detective downed the shot and motioned for another, which Red graciously obliged.

"Somebody came in and said Shady was dead," the bartender said. "They were saying you did it."

"Would that bother you?" Martel asked. "Having a murderer across the bar?"

Red shrugged.

"I've served worse," he said. "Besides, as far as I'm concerned, humans killing humans is a helluva start..."

Martel drank the second shot slower than the first.

"Somebody else killed Shady," he said, "but they used Maxwell to do it."

"Well, I never saw the need for guns myself," Red replied, showing off his fists, "not when I have *these*." He reached behind the bar and pulled out an oversized meat cleaver. "Also, *this*..."

Red took a hack at the top of the bar, leaving the blade buried in the wood. Martel leaned back on his stool.

"So, what happened?" the bartender asked, pouring more whiskey.

Extending his arm as far as he could, Martel retrieved the shot glass.

"I went to see Gelatinous Bob," he said, "and asked him some questions about my case."

"He hates being called that."

"So I gathered," Martel replied. "He slipped me a mickey and I woke up in the Boneyards."

"What about Shady?"

"He was lying next to me with half his head blown off."

"Sure you didn't do it?" Red asked.

Martel finished the drink and set the glass upside down on the bar.

"Of course not!" he said. "There were two shots fired from Maxwell. They killed Shady with the first and probably put the gun in my hand for the second, just so the residue was on my skin."

"Seems like they went to a lot of trouble just for calling him *Bob*."

"Maybe," Martel said, not sure if Red was being facetious, "but I think he didn't like the questions I was asking."

"So, why aren't you still in jail?" Red asked.

"My client got me out."

"Must be nice to be human," Red replied. "I'd still be rotting in my cell."

"He also gave me more work to do," Martel went on, oblivious to the bartender's comment. "There's a missing lord he wants me to find."

"Well, good luck with that..."

For the first time, Martel became dimly aware of someone else in the Sous-Sol. Behind him, he spotted a tall, dark shape in one of the booths. In the flickering light of the candle on the table, Mister Munge's burned face appeared in and out of the shadows.

"What is Munge doing here?" Martel asked Red.

The bartender shrugged. "Louis hired him."

"For what?"

"Bouncer."

Martel's eyebrow went up. "There's never anybody in here to bounce..."

"What can I tell you?" Red replied, losing patience. "I guess Louis felt sorry for the bastard now that the Griefers are kaput."

Since hearing the news about Kid being killed, Martel hadn't had much time to process the repercussions, but seeing Munge in the bar would not have been one of them. The detective crossed the room and sat across the booth from the newly minted bouncer.

"Sorry about Kid," Martel said, lying out of courtesy.

Munge grumbled something unintelligible.

"But at least you got a job here," Martel said, "for some reason..."

"Munge grateful."

"Maybe it's the whiskey talking but if you're looking for extra work, I might have a job for you."

Munge stayed silent, but Martel was keenly away of the man's eyes burning into him.

"I lost Maxwell recently," the detective continued, "so I could use someone with a little muscle in case things go sideways."

"You want Munge as enforcer?"

Martel coughed into his hand. "Let's just say *bodyguard* for now."

To his surprise, Martel watched as a smile cracked the seared face across the booth.

In the southern part of the West End, Saint Eligius Royal Hospital rose like a brick monolith of mercy and medical expertise. St. Eligius catered exclusively to the rich and powerful of Imperial society, including the Emperor's own family. When Prince Richard arrived at the maternity ward late in the day, the head nursebot accosted him with multiple mechanical arms flailing in the air.

"Lady Lilith is already in the delivery room!" the egg-shaped robot shouted, hovering a few feet off the ground. "We need you to scrub up immediately!"

Richard followed in a daze, his eyes overstimulated by noises and faces blurring past him. Leading him into a small alcove, the nursebot directed the prince to roll up his shirt and stick his arms into a pair of sleeve-like devices. After flashes of ultraviolet light sterilized his skin, Richard removed his arms and donned gloves and a medical gown. Moments later, he was standing in a delivery room like a surreal dreamscape. Wires and cords stretched to infinity, and faceless people filled the room like ghosts.

"Over here," someone said weakly.

Richard recognized the voice coming from the person lying on the table, but both the tone and seeing Lilith's ashen face created such a discrepancy in his mind that he could not bring himself to believe what he saw or heard.

"Get over here!" Lilith repeated, promptly removing any doubt.

Richard appeared at her side as if carried across the room by her will alone. A sheet hanging across her chest served as a barrier between Lilith and what the medical staff were doing, providing a degree of privacy between the patient and her husband.

"How are you feeling?" Richard asked.

"I've been in labor for hours," Lilith replied. "How do you think?"

"I'm sorry," he said. "My father wanted to berate me about the conclave. He thinks I should withdraw my nomination..."

She stared at him. "And what did *you* say?"

"I said I'd think about it."

Lilith screamed, sending Richard backwards on his heels.

"The baby's coming!" one of the doctors shouted.

"Come closer," Lilith said, biting her lip. Richard hesitated but leaned his ear as close as he dared, slightly concerned she might bite it off. On the contrary, however, her voice was soft.

"I've been thinking about his name," she said, nearly whispering.

"Yes?"

"I'd like us to name him Mason, after my father..."

Richard nodded. "That's a good name."

From the other side of the cloth partition, the doctor said, "Push!"

Lilith closed her eyes, the strain apparent on her face.

"One more time," the doctor said. "Push!"

Richard saw his wife sacrificing every ounce of her strength, and then the burden lifted and her face turned calm.

"He's out," the doctor said, and the delivery room filled with the wailing of a baby's cry.

Richard peered over the partition and caught a glimpse of his son, covered in blood. He turned back to his wife, but her eyes were still closed. Over the screams of the baby, alarms began sounding.

"She's hemorrhaging!" someone yelled.

A nurse, a human this time, pushed Richard out of the room and told him to wait. After more than an hour, the same nurse reappeared and handed him a baby wrapped in a towel. At the same time, the doctor came out of the delivery room to tell the prince that Lady Lilith was dead.

Prince Richard held his son, a tiny pink face surrounded by white terrycloth. No one could have been more vulnerable or more needing of protection. At that moment, Richard made a vow he intended to keep no matter what happened.

"I will keep you safe," he said.

CHAPTER TEN

Family members and dignitaries gathered at the Fogmore Gardens for the funeral of Lady Lilith Augustus. Fogmore was adjacent to the Palace estate and contained the mausoleums for each of the Five Families. Even so, the Emperor did not attend. Lady Veber wondered how Prince Richard felt about his father's absence.

Dressed in black, Lady Veber sat quietly alone in the chapel where the funeral service was being held. The rest of the pews were filled with people, and a few robots. Lord Tagus III had brought his own, the one named Burkebot.

What a curious pair they make, Lady Veber thought. *Perhaps a robot is the only friend Tagus still has...*

Lord Devlin Maycare was in attendance, along with his current girlfriend, Lady Candice Woodwick. Lady Veber had known Maycare for many years, and Candy had been best friends with Lilith.

What a small world it was, these tight circles of nobility. Everybody knew each other and loathed one another more often than not.

Lady Veber took another glance at Tagus.

Prince Richard spoke at the podium, talking about how much he missed his wife and how important their son Mason had been to her. Lady Candice was crying by the end of the speech, but Lady Veber's own eyes remained dry. She had lost enough tears when her son Philip had died, and she had no intention of losing more.

After the service, Lady Veber caught Prince Richard near the large picture of Lilith beside her coffin.

"My condolences," she said, touching his hand. "How is little Mason?"

The prince pulled his hand away, perhaps a bit too abruptly.

"He's well," he replied. "I thought it best to leave him at the palace."

"Of course," Lady Veber said. "A funeral is no place for a baby."

"With Tagus here, it's better to be safe than sorry."

"I'm surprised he came," Lady Veber remarked, "but I doubt he'd pose a danger to a child..."

"You can never tell," Richard replied. "He's capable of anything."

Lady Veber saw a glimmer of paranoia in Richard's gaze, but thought better than making a point of it. Nevertheless, she knew she might not have another chance to press him about the conclave.

"Have you thought more about your nomination?" she asked.

"Yes," he said firmly. "The nomination *stands*."

"Are you expecting me to support it?"

"If you did," he replied, "I would protect you from Tagus."

"Who says I need protecting?" Lady Veber asked.

"From Tagus, we all do," the prince said. "We *all* do."

Lady Veber left him alone but encountered Lord Tagus himself outside the chapel. His robot was standing awkwardly behind him.

"Did you talk any sense into him?" Tagus asked gruffly.

"Apparently not," she replied.

"Such a damn fool," Tagus remarked, "but it doesn't change anything. I fully expect to be the next emperor..."

"Do you?"

"Assuming you remember our arrangement," Tagus said. "Your vote and a vote from the Groens will assure my victory. Of course, if you vote against me, I cannot guarantee what would happen *next*."

"That sounds suspiciously like a threat," Lady Veber said.

"I don't care what it sounds like," Tagus replied. "I won't overlook another slight from your family."

Turning on his heel, Tagus walked away without another word. His robot gave a short bow and then followed.

Staring at the bottle on his desk, Thomas Martel was wondering how early was too early to start drinking when Dolores' Long Island accent broke the silence.

"There's a young man out here to see ya!" she yelled through the wall separating Martel from the front of the office. "How old are ya, hon?"

"Sixteen," Martel heard someone say.

"Oh ma gawd, he's such a cutie!" Dolores remarked. "Your mutha must be so proud!"

"I never knew my mother," the voice said.

"Aw, ya poor de-ah!"

Teenagers in Ashetown were usually trouble, either throwing bricks through windows or stealing gravcars. When Martel was still a police detective, he turned his back on a group of delinquents only to have them hotwire the gravcar he shared with Detective Crawley, his old partner. Crawley was so furious that by the time he rounded up all the underage boys in the neighborhood, the police department cells looked like the *Lord of the Flies*.

Martel slipped the bottle into a desk drawer and went to the front. Just as Dolores had described him, the boy was young and handsome, much different than the kids around here.

"What can I do for you?" Martel asked.

"My name is Roland," he said. "I'm told you're looking for Radford Groen."

"What's it to you?" the detective asked.

"Sorry," the boy replied sheepishly. "I go by Roland, but my given name is Jack Groen. Radford is my uncle..."

Martel's expression softened. "Is that so?"

"I was adopted after my parents died," Roland went on, "but I've been trying to make contact with my birth family."

"Who told you I was looking for your uncle?"

"Lady Candice called me and said you were working on the case," Roland replied.

"Lady Candice?"

"Yes," Roland said. "Have you met her?"

"Can't say I have," Martel said.

"She's beautiful!" Dolores remarked, her voice coming from the box on the front desk. "She and Lord Maycare are in all the tabloids!"

"Why are you looking at tabloids?" Martel asked her.

"I got a lot of free time," she replied. "Ya know, while I'm waitin' for clients to come through the dawr."

Martel's narrowed eyes left the box on the desk and focused on the boy.

"Listen, kid," the detective said, "I just don't see how you can help me look for your uncle."

A fly, which had wandered in through an open window, meandered close to Roland who, with a nearly imperceptible motion, snatched it out of the air, holding the tiny insect between his thumb and forefinger. Martel noticed the fly was alive, its wings still buzzing.

"My adoptive mother trained me well," Roland said, releasing the fly unharmed.

Martel took a moment but nodded.

"Well, I just hired someone," he said, thinking of Munge, "but I guess you could tag along..."

The box on the desk nearly beamed.
"So proud of ya!" Dolores said.

Mister Munge shared his attic apartment with a number of cats, although he didn't entirely know how many. When he woke in the morning, he lay on his left side, relegated to the far edge of the bed. Cats took up the rest of the real estate, some huddled together on the bed in groups of two or three while others balanced precariously on Munge himself. Any thoughts of rolling over or shifting his weight were mere fantasies, the thing of dreams before he rose in the morning.

Munge stirred and the cats sleeping on him bounded off, disturbing the other cats on the bed. A great howling ensued as everyone knew feeding time was nigh. His left arm still asleep, Munge shook it until the sensation of needles slowly subsided. Meanwhile, cats crowded around his feet now on the cold floor, rubbing against his ankles in feigned fidelity to their kibble god.

Munge groaned when he stood up, partly due to the stiff muscles in his back and partially due to the Russian Blue hanging by her claws on Munge's shoulder. He crossed the short distance from the bed to the kitchen, the cat dangling the whole way, and opened one of the cupboards. The chorus of meows rose in both octaves and tempo while Munge removed several cans, laboriously opening each one.

He set bowls of food on the floor only to see his forearms disappear in a sea of fur and swishing tails. Munge sometimes wondered if they would go after his hands instead, preferring his flesh from whatever meat they usually devoured. He had resigned himself to the thought that, upon his death, the cats would feast on his body until the authorities finally investigated the smell.

Careful not to step on anyone, Munge walked gingerly across the floor again, headed this time for the litter boxes in the other corner of the attic. A loud banging came from below, sharp tapping as if from the end of a broom handle. An old woman's voice shouted up through the floorboards.

"Quiet up there!" Munge's landlady yelled. "Stop clomping around like an elephant!"

"Munge sorry!" he replied.

"And don't forget the rent!"

He cringed, knowing he could no longer count on the pittance that Kid Vicious had paid him. Even as Kid's enforcer, Munge's pay was barely enough to cover expenses, and now he depended on his job at the Sous-Sol and whatever Thomas Martel would shell out. Kitty litter alone was half his paycheck...

A faint buzzing came from his datapad on the nightstand.

Retrieving the device, Munge forgot about one of the ceiling beams, catching him in the forehead. Although in pain, he was more concerned about any cats possibly perched on his shoulders. Thankfully, all of the cats, however many there might have been, were still busy grooming themselves in an after-breakfast frenzy on the floor.

On the datapad, Martel's face appeared.

"Are you all right?" he asked, apparently seeing Munge massaging his temple.

"Munge okay."

"I've got some work for you," the detective went on. "Can you meet me in the West End?"

"Yes," he replied. "Send Munge address."

Martel's face vanished, replaced by a text message of the location. Munge read it with a sense of satisfaction, knowing he could now afford another shipment of kitty litter.

The life of Lord Eugene "Ducky" Davenport was not an easy one. For example, after a night on the town, those early tee times were murder. Thankfully, he had a steady supply of Lotus petals to help him through. After getting home in the wee hours of the night, a petal dissolved on the tongue and a few hours of sleep gave Ducky all the rest he needed. Of course, that didn't mean he wouldn't ingest another petal after eighteen holes at the Greenwood Country Club. A mid-afternoon nap and a few dreams later, Ducky was his chipper self again. Sometimes, after an especially stressful dinner at the club, he might eat more petals as the evening progressed, but Ducky was of the opinion that you can never have too much of a good thing.

Ducky had noticed, however, that his Lotus supply was no longer lasting a full week, so he decided to buy more the next time he saw his connection...

In an exclusive salon in the West End, Ducky soaked his weary feet in a bath of warm water while a mani-pedibot worked on his fingernails. Delicate tools at the end of the robot's arms gently treated Ducky's cuticles while Ducky lay semi-reclined in a chair. His eyes were closed, but he cracked them just a sliver when the glass door at the front of the salon opened and two men walked in.

Technically, one was a rumply-dressed man while the other was more of a teenager.

Opening his eyes wider, Ducky became concerned when the two newcomers came directly toward him.

Am I being mugged? Ducky thought. His first instinct was to run, but his feet still needed a few minutes to soak.

For her part, the mani-pedibot disappeared through a curtain into the back room.

Ducky raised his hands. "I don't have any money."

Both men stopped, their faces perplexed, before the older one stepped forward.

"Actually," he said, "I'm here to thank you."

"Really?" Ducky replied, lowering his hands. "What for?"

"You recommended me to Lord Maycare," he said.

"You're not my podiatrist," Ducky remarked.

"No, I'm Thomas Martel, the *private detective*."

"Oh, of course!" Ducky said. "Silly me..."

Martel motioned toward the younger man. "This is Jack Groen, Lord Radford Groen's nephew..."

"I see," Ducky replied. "Well, you seem better put together than your poor uncle, I must say."

"Thank you?" the boy said.

"I mean, let's be honest," Ducky went on, "he's a bit of a mess..."

"About Lord Groen," Martel said. "We'd like to ask you a few questions if you don't mind."

"Why is that?" Ducky asked.

"He's gone missing," the detective replied.

"Well, *I* certainly don't know where he is."

"It's our understanding that you've been supplying him with Lotus," Martel said, leaning a bit closer than Ducky would have liked.

"I don't know what you mean..."

"Lord Woodwick witnessed you giving him petals at the horse track."

"Winnie is a professional lush," Ducky said. "I wouldn't believe a word he says."

Martel leaned even closer, his breath smelling of alcohol.

"Listen," he said grimly. "We know you've been supplying Lotus to bigwigs all over town, which means you've been getting it from somewhere. Now, we just need you to tell us where, and maybe we can find Uncle Groen in the process."

Ducky did his level best to sit straight in his reclining chair. "And if I refuse?"

Martel tilted his head toward the salon entrance.

"Then the man outside will come inside," he said. "And you won't like that very much."

Ducky glanced at the glass front of the salon. On the sidewalk, a large shape loomed against the window, its eyes blazing like hellfire. Ducky was not entirely sure whether he was human or not, but his face was horribly burned, probably from something hell-related.

Ducky swallowed hard.

"What do you want to know?" he asked.

The Psi Lords were a data cartel, gathering and selling information around the Imperium. No one in the organization knew the innate value of information more than Kanet Solan, and once he heard what Ta Demona had found, he knew just what to do with it.

He even had special incense for the occasion.

"Cinnamon?" Demona asked.

Solan pushed the incense stick into a container of sand and lit the tip. Wafts of smoke carrying the scent of aromatic spices drifted through the chamber.

"Cinnamon attracts wealth and power," he said. "Or so I'm told..."

"And you believe that?"

"It also smells like apple pie," Solan replied.

Demona crossed her arms. The filter mask covering most of her face made a mechanical noise as she breathed in the air, but Solan doubted she could appreciate the aroma.

"True or not," he went on, "I'm confident our guest will find it pleasing."

Demona stayed silent, but Solan could easily read what she was thinking.

You don't approve? he thought.

No, she replied telepathically.

"Why is that?" Solan asked aloud.

"We had a deal with the boy," she replied.

"And we kept it," Solan said, taking a seat on one of the oversized pillows in the room. "We found his parents and told young Roland what had happened to them."

"But we now know that information wasn't *accurate*," Demona said, her eyes blazing against her green skin.

Solan waved his hand dismissively.

"Roland could only pay us with the promise of a future favor," Solan said. "We will gain more financially by selling this new information than what we could have expected to earn from the boy. Consider this his favor being paid... albeit *indirectly*."

"By withholding it from him?" Demona asked.

"I dare say he'll learn soon enough," Solan said with a laugh.

"What do you mean?"

"Well," he explained, "if we know our guest like I think we do, Roland may find himself in danger."

Her anger flashed across Solan's mind.

"Don't tell me you're developing scruples?" he asked. "We sell information, not morality, Ta."

"Maybe so," she replied, "but withholding information from one client to sell to another damages our credibility."

"Let me worry about our credibility," Solan said, growing stern. "Your role is to find the information, not determine what to do with it."

He sensed her thoughts recoil.

"Now, now," he said, softening his tone. "You have nothing to worry about... provided you know your *place*."

Someone else was coming. Solan felt her fear as well, although those thoughts were clouded more with confusion like someone lost.

"Our guest has arrived," Solan said, motioning for Demona to leave.

Demona bowed and disappeared behind a curtain concealing a hidden door. On the opposite side of the room, from a tunnel leading to the surface, the form of a woman emerged, dressed in a hooded robe. Lowering the hood, she revealed a regal face with tightly braided hair.

"Lady Veber," Solan said, getting to his feet. "So happy to finally meet you."

The apartment that Lord Radford Groen shared with Lord Winsor Woodwick included a balcony with a view of the West End. Resting in a chair, Groen watched the birds fluttering through the morning sky, their graceful motions a relaxing respite from the drug-fueled nightmares he had endured while still under the influence of Lotus.

It's good to be free from the petals, he thought, taking a sip of Mimosa from a tall, fluted glass.

Woodwick came out on the balcony with a tray, setting it down on a table beside his roommate. Groen returned the Mimosa to the tray, surveying what Winnie had brought him.

"I hope your stomach can tolerate some eggs," Woodwick said.

"We'll soon find out..." Groen replied, taking the plate and utensils.

"I say, Radford, it's so good to have you back!" Woodwick gushed, despite himself. "I was so worried!"

Groen shrugged between mouthfuls. "I'm not a man that stays down for long."

"Do you want your datapad?" Woodwick asked. "The horses at Mudderfield are running today."

"Right," Groen replied. "I should put my bets in before the races start..."

Woodwick vanished back into the apartment but continued talking.

"Candy will be delighted you're doing better," Woodwick's muffled voice was saying. "Perhaps you could take that boy with you as well."

"Who?" Groen shouted back.

"Your nephew," Woodwick replied. "*Jack Groen.*"

The plate slipped out of Groen's hands, catching the edge of the deck chair and scattering eggs across the balcony. He swallowed what was left in his mouth as he stood and went inside.

Woodwick was still retrieving the datapad from the living room when Groen passed through the apartment toward his bedroom.

"Where are you going?" Woodwick asked.

Without answering, Groen opened his bedroom door. Stepping inside, he found a woman in a nightgown lying on his bed. Even partially covered by a sheet, she was clearly many months pregnant.

Woodwick peered into the room, the datapad in his hands. "Who the devil is *she*?"

"Josephine," Groen whispered.

"Well, this isn't cricket!" Woodwick complained. "I had no idea you were having a *guest*!"

Groen shut the bedroom door in his roommate's face. From the other side, Woodwick muttered "Humph!"

Groen went to the bed.

"What are you doing here?" he asked.

"There's something I need to tell you," she replied earnestly, taking his hand. "Something terrible has happened."

"What is it?"

"The baby isn't Robert's," she said.

"Don't be absurd!" Groen replied.

Tears swelled in Josephine's eyes. "It's true."

"How... why?"

"I feel so guilty," she said, "but he didn't give me a choice."

From the adjoining bathroom, a man appeared in the doorway. Older than Groen or Josephine, he wore a black and gold tunic. His name was Lord Rupert Tagus II, patriarch of the Tagus family and father to Tagus III.

"*Droit du seigneur*," he said. "The lord's right."

"What the hell are you talking about?" Groen asked angrily.

"Your miserable family owes everything to mine," Tagus replied with disdain. "Without the house of Tagus, the Groens would be *nothing*!"

"He said he would destroy Robert if I didn't sleep with him," Josephine said.

"Of course," Tagus remarked, "I didn't expect her to get *pregnant...*"

"You're a monster," Groen said.

"Perhaps," Tagus said, "but at least I had fun in the process."

Groen lunged at the old man, putting his hands around Tagus' thin neck and squeezing at hard as he could. Behind him, Groen heard Josephine scream and then felt her shaking him.

"Uncle Radford!" she shouted. "Uncle Radford!"

Groen opened his eyes and found a young man standing over him, jostling him roughly as he lay in a cot.

"Wake up, Uncle Radford," the boy said. "We're going to take you home."

The haze of dreams still spinning in his head, Groen did his best to sit up. In the background, he could swear he saw a large man with a burned face throwing a gangster against a wall. Another man, this one with dark skin, appeared at the boy's side.

"Come on, Roland," the man said. "We need to go."

The two of them pulled Groen from the cot, each one taking an arm. Groen turned his head weakly toward the younger man.

"Who are you?" he asked.

The boy smiled.

"I'm your nephew," he said. "You can call me *Jack*."

CHAPTER ELEVEN

Doctors, doctors, and more doctors. They came in groups and alone, but none of them could tell Lady Veber what was killing her son, Philip.

Whichever doctor was currently treating her son was hovering uselessly outside Philip's room. Lady Veber found him assessing his charts and looking bewildered, no help to anyone. In his bedroom, her son lay under blankets, surrounded by Lady Veber's handmaidens watching over him. His brown eyes were sunken like someone three times his age. His once beautiful hair was stringy and damp from days of fever.

On the day Philip died, Lady Veber found her son standing alone in his chambers, having sent everyone away. She put a hand on his shoulder, feeling the bones protruding beneath the linen of his night clothes.

"You feel cold as ice," she said.

She would always remember how Philip gave a little laugh right before his mouth twisted.

"What's the matter?" she asked.

"I feel funny," Philip replied, his words slurring.

Lady Veber ran to fetch the doctor. When they returned, Philip lay convulsing on the floor. With the help of a nursebot, they got the boy back into his room where his body contorted on the bed and his eyes rolled back into his skull. The doctor nearly shoved Lady Veber through the bedroom doorway even as she insisted that she wanted to stay.

"Lady Veber, please!" he had shouted.

When the door slid shut, the last thing Lady Veber saw of her son was his face drained of blood. After many minutes had passed, the door opened.

Her son was dead.

Roland, otherwise known as Jack Groen, waited at his uncle's bedside while Lord Radford Groen slept restlessly, the pillow soaked with sweat. Roland leaned over the bed, careful not to tip the bucket on the floor, and exchanged the compress on his uncle's head with a cold one.

Groen opened his eyes.

"Am I dreaming?" he asked weakly.

"No," Roland replied. "We found you at a Lotus den in Ashetown. Do you remember us rescuing you?"

Groen took a moment, but then nodded. "Yes."

"Do you know who I am?" Roland asked.

Groen's bloodshot eyes turned to the boy.

"You're Josephine's son," he said.

"That's right," Roland replied. "I'm Josephine and Robert Groen's son."

Groen started to disagree, but Lord Winsor Woodwick came barging into the room.

"I thought I heard voices!" he said, his walrus mustache twitching excitedly.

"He's awake," Roland confirmed.

"Calm down, Winnie," Groen said.

"I dare say, Radford, I've been positively gutted since you went missing," Woodwick replied. "I've been self-medicating with gin and sedatives..."

"I had a dream about you," Groen said. "You made me eggs."

"Rubbish!" Woodwick replied. "You know I've never set foot in the kitchen!"

"I guess I should've known it was a dream."

"Don't you worry, old chap," Woodwick said. "We'll have you well again in no time."

Roland felt his uncle's eyes on him, but Groen looked away when the boy returned his gaze.

"Listen, Winnie," Groen said after a long pause, "I wonder if you could leave me alone with my nephew for a few minutes? I want to talk to him..."

"Well, I don't see why *I* can't be present," Woodwick replied with annoyance, "but as you *like*."

The lord shuffled out of the bedroom in a huff. Groen motioned to his nephew to close the door. Once he had done so, Roland returned to his uncle's bedside.

"What is it?" the boy asked.

"How much do you know about your parents?" Groen replied.

"Not very much," Roland said. "I know they were killed and I was taken by the man who killed them. It wasn't until recently that I even knew who they were."

"Robert was my cousin," Groen said, "but Josephine and I had been friends long before the two were married."

"You were?"

"Robert was always jealous of us. He even accused me of being your real father."

"Were you?" Roland asked.

"Of course not," Groen said, "but Robert was not far off as it turned out."

"What do you mean?"

"Robert was indeed *not* your father."

Groen coughed several times until Roland gave him a drink of water from the glass on the nightstand.

"Are you all right?" the boy asked.

"Never mind that," Groen replied. "There's something you need to know but it can't leave this room. If it did, there's no telling what danger you'd be in."

Roland stayed silent.

"After she became pregnant with you," Roland said, "Josephine confided in me that someone had forced himself on her."

Roland's face reddened while his heart pounded in his chest. "Who was it?"

After another long pause, as if Roland's uncle was afraid to say the words, he answered.

"Rupert Tagus II," Groen said.

When Thomas Martel arrived at the Maycare estate, Benson the butlerbot once again asked for the detective's weapon before proceeding. Martel opened his coat, revealing an empty holster.

"Maxwell is in police custody," he said.

Martel couldn't be sure, but thought the robot's face showed a hint of disappointment.

"Do you like guns?" the detective asked.

"As a feat of engineering, yes," Benson replied. "As a tool for killing, *no*."

Instead of Maycare's study, the butlerbot brought Martel out onto a terrace facing a wide expanse of grass. Lord Devlin Maycare was taking swings with a golf club, launching the little white balls into the green space.

"Is that some kind of park?" Martel asked.

Maycare, appearing not to understand the question at first, laughed.

"A park?" he said. "That's my backyard!"

Martel wondered if he was charging Maycare enough.

"Thanks for coming in person," Maycare went on. "I was hoping you could give me an update on the hypersled situation."

Removing a datapad from his coat, Martel showed him an image of Jollux on the screen.

"This is the loan shark I think is involved," the detective explained. "He seemed pretty touchy about it when I raised the subject. Also, he tried to frame me for murder..."

Maycare lobbed another golf ball into the backyard. Benson had left the terrace and was collecting the balls in the grass with a bucket.

"I'm sorry about that," Maycare said, referring to the detective's legal issues. "My lawyer says he can get it dismissed. It'll just take some time."

"I have to admit," Martel replied, "I feel a little naked without Maxwell hanging from my shoulder."

From inside the house, a woman with blond hair and a pink tennis outfit came out to join them. Her blue, expressive eyes grew larger when she saw the detective.

"Mister Martel!" she shouted, throwing her arms around him. Her perfume smelled of lilacs.

"Hello?" the detective stuttered, glancing at Maycare for help.

"This is Lady Candice Woodwick," Maycare said.

"You can call me *Candy*," she added, releasing him and taking a step back. Martel felt she was still a bit too close.

"Jack Groen mentioned you..." the detective said.

"Isn't he a charmer?" she remarked, "but anyway, I wanted to thank you for finding Lord Groen. My Uncle Winnie was worried sick!"

"It was no problem," Martel replied. "Jack was a big help."

She gave Maycare a coy look.

"Devlin's lucky he already snatched me up," she said, "otherwise I might have given Jack a second look."

Maycare laughed, but then said, "What?"

"Don't worry," Candy replied. "He's too young."

Maycare knelt to place another golf ball on the tee.

"And penniless," he said before taking a powerful swing.

Martel heard a loud, metallic *plunk!* and saw Benson rubbing the side of his head in the yard.

"Sorry!" Maycare shouted.

"With Lord Groen back," Martel asked Candy, "I suppose the two of you will be back at Mudderfield Downs?"

"Why is that?" Candy replied.

"Jack said you and his uncle enjoy betting on the races," Martel said.

"Oh, that silly boy!" she laughed. "The things he says..."

Candy gave the detective a wide smile and went back into the house.

Magnus Black and his ship, the *Starling*, dropped out of hyperspace at pre-arranged coordinates in deep space, far from prying eyes. The *Starling* was shaped like an arrowhead with short, thick wings on either side of the main fuselage. Magnus peered from the cockpit perched high at the front of the ship, giving him a perfect view of the luxury yacht waiting for him.

Firing twin thrusters, Magnus brought his ship around the side of the yacht, pairing it with the other vessel's airlock. When the hatch opened, a burly crewman stood on the other side, his white uniform trimmed with a turquoise stripe down each pant leg.

"This way," the crewman said with an air of refinement suggesting he was normally used to dealing with more dignified guests.

The interior of the yacht was reminiscent of a royal estate, the walls painted in shades of white and pale blue. Tiles, with ceramic scallops, ran along the corridors and decorated doorways. A newcomer might have been impressed by such adornments, but this was not Magnus' first time on the ship.

The crewman stopped and entered a code to open a sliding door. Magnus went inside, leaving the crewman to remain in the hallway as the door slid shut again.

Lady Veber, resting on one of the chairs in her chambers, welcomed the assassin.

"I'm glad you got my message," she said.

"I never turn down a job," Magnus replied, "if the money's right."

"I assume the circumstances are more agreeable *this* time," she said.

"Last time I was your prisoner," Magnus said, "so I'd say it's an improvement."

Lady Veber left her seat and came closer, but not too close, to the killer.

"When I saw you last," she said, "you were helping me poison Rupert Tagus II. I don't remember if I ever thanked you for that."

"Your payment was all the thanks I needed."

"I'm headed to Lokeren," she replied, changing the subject. "I'm to reconvene the Imperial Conclave..."

"I don't follow politics," Magnus remarked.

"I wish I had that luxury," Lady Veber said, "but sadly I'm very much in the middle of things, as usual."

Magnus said nothing.

"How much do you know of Rupert Tagus III?" she asked.

"Only that he's a dick like his father."

Lady Veber laughed.

"And then some," she replied. "Sometimes I think we killed the wrong Tagus, but that's neither here nor there--"

"Why am I here?" Magnus interrupted, getting to the point. "Do you want me to kill another Tagus?"

"In a manner of speaking," she replied, "but just not *that* one."

"Who then?"

"It's recently come to my attention," she said, "that Rupert Tagus Senior had a bastard son, by way of the Groen family, named Jack Groen." After a pause, she said, "He's only a teenager. Is that going to be a problem for you?"

"No," Magnus replied.

"Good."

"It's none of my business," Magnus said, "but why the kid and not the dick?"

Lady Veber took a deep breath and sighed.

"Because when the Tagus family killed my son," she said, "he was about the same age as Jack Groen is now."

"Interesting," Magnus replied.

Lady Veber turned away from him.

"I know," she said, "but I can't sleep knowing Rupert's bastard son is walking alive while my son is dead. I can't explain it. I just need it *done*."

"Understood," Magnus replied.

At the Tagus family estate, built like a Victorian mansion, Rupert Tagus III slept in the master bedroom in the same four-poster bed as his father and his father's father before him.

Lost in sleep, Tagus dreamed of walking through the hallways of the estate, the dark wood of the walls and floors encroaching on him like the throat of a monster. He passed portraits of former patriarchs along the way. They watched him stroll past, their eyes disapproving.

Tagus stopped at a door. Opening it, he entered the great hall where state dinners were normally held. Now the tables and chairs were pushed to the edges of the room.

"Happy birthday, Rupert!" someone shouted and suddenly Tagus was ten years old, running toward a group of other children gathered at the center of the hall. Presents were stacked in an orderly pile around a table where a cake with ten candles was sitting. Kids from all the major families were there, waiting for the birthday boy.

"Blow out your candles!" a girl shouted.

Tagus, short for his age, lifted himself on tiptoes and inhaled, but before he could extinguish the little points of light, a larger boy blew them out instead.

"Richard!" Tagus yelled, scowling at the other child.

The Augustus boy laughed.

"Too slow!" Richard said with a shrug. "Do better next time!"

Tagus stomped out of the great hall in a huff, careful that no one would see the tears forming in his eyes. Safely in the corridor, he had transformed back into an adult again.

Farther along the passageway, another door beckoned. After the previous one, Tagus hesitated to turn the knob, but he felt compelled, so he went inside anyway. Now he was a cadet in the Naval Academy, his light blue uniform pressed and starched. His father sat behind the desk in his office. The patriarch had more hair then, but it had already started turning gray.

Tagus stepped forward, the deep expanse of the oak desk between him and his father.

"It's an outrage!" Tagus shouted. "They had no right to pick Augustus over you!"

"I agree," his father said, "but Hector is now the Emperor."

"How can you just sit there?" Tagus asked. "We must *do* something!"

"What do you suggest, boy?" his father replied. "The conclave has voted, and we lost."

Tagus' face turned a deep crimson. "I'll think of something..."

"Calm yourself," the patriarch said. "That temper of yours will be your undoing."

"I'm a soldier, not a politician," Tagus retorted. "We can't sit idly by while the other houses treat us like this!"

His father chuckled.

"You're a boy playing soldier," he said, "but you're right about one thing."

"Yes?"

"We won't let this slight go unanswered," the patriarch replied, "but we'll do it *my* way."

The office dissolved into the estate's parlor, a fireplace in the corner alight with a bright flame. Tagus' father, now much older, was sitting on a couch beside a platter of tea and cookies. Lady Veber stood with her arms crossed.

The patriarch set a teacup down before taking a bite out of a cookie. Standing to the side, Tagus saw Lady Veber smile.

"She poisoned you," Tagus told his father.

The patriarch stared down at himself, his body slowly beginning to fade.

"It would seem so," he replied.

"I will avenge you," Tagus said. "I don't care what I promised Lady Veber..."

"Careful, boy," his father warned. "She's more dangerous than you can imagine."

"Why?"

"Because," the patriarch said, just before dissolving into nothing, "she has nothing to lose."

Tagus woke, entangled in silk sheets.

Roland woke in his own bed, having spent the last few days largely at the bedside of his uncle. At breakfast with his adoptive mother Lefty Lucy, Roland couldn't help but think about what his uncle had said.

He could barely eat the grilled fish Lucy had made for him, which did not go unnoticed.

"Sorry," he said, careful not to meet her stern gaze. "I'm not very hungry."

She poured miso soup into a bowl.

"It's just," Roland went on, "it's a little hard to believe, don't you think?"

Lucy placed a spoon next to the soup.

"And what about the Psi Lords?" the boy said. "That woman with the green skin said Robert Groen was my father. Could the Psi Lords have been wrong?"

Lucy's eyes again fixed on the boy.

"Then why would they lie?" he asked.

His adoptive mother curled her legs under the low table and set about her own breakfast. Her movements were fluid and precise, wasting nothing.

"I'll go see Detective Martel!" Roland said suddenly. "Maybe he can find out something?"

Lucy continued eating her breakfast in silence.

A few hours later, Roland was back in Ashetown, walking from the transmat station to Martel's office several blocks away. Although the distance was not far, the neighborhood, like much of the district, was seedy and run-down. Passing an ANDI's grocery store painted with gang signs, Roland could just make out the noise of polka music coming from inside. In the display window, taped over in places where it had cracked, a monitor showed a VOX newscast with Sylvia Flax on the screen:

"The latest reports from Lokeren," she said, "say the Imperial Conclave has reconvened and a vote will take place in the coming days. In other news, the Lotus epidemic has reached the highest levels of society with even members of the nobility succumbing to the chem's addictive qualities. The Emperor was unavailable for comment..."

Roland, who had stopped to watch, started again toward Martel's office, but halted when he heard a disturbance from the adjoining alley. Poking his head around the corner, he saw two men and an orange general-purpose robot. The genbot's left arm hung loosely from its socket.

"What's going on here?" Roland asked, stepping into the alley.

The two men turned to face the boy. One wore torn pants and a soiled jacket while the other held a greasy wrench. Both men had bloodshot eyes that stared at Roland with desperate ferocity.

"What's it to you?" the one with the wrench asked.

"Help me, sir," the orange robot pleaded. "These Lotus eaters attacked me for no reason!"

"Is that right?" Roland asked.

The man in the ripped pants pointed at the genbot. "We're going to sell him for parts."

Roland moved farther into the alley and motioned with his thumb toward the street.

"Get out of here, genbot," he said.

Giving the other two a wide berth, the robot made it to the sidewalk and started running without looking back. The other two turned their attention squarely on Roland.

"You made a big mistake," the man with the torn pants said, as he and his companion approached the boy.

Roland spread his feet apart, holding his left arm and fist close to his body while his right arm stretched in front of him. Although the boy knew the stance was impressive, even he was surprised by how quickly the two chem junkies stopped in their tracks. Roland saw the terror in their eyes and watched the one man drop his wrench to the ground.

That was easy, Roland thought.

The Lotus eaters ran in the opposite direction, dashing down the alley and out the other end. Roland smiled, relaxing his stance before turning back toward the street. When he did so, he came face to face with a man standing behind him.

Wearing a dark leather coat, the man carried a blaster in his hand. His hair was shaved to a fine stubble. Seeing the man's icy stare, Roland felt his blood turn cold.

CHAPTER TWELVE

Magnus Black sized up Jack Groen, the boy standing alone in the alley. As Lady Veber had warned, the boy was young, but Magnus had killed young men before. He motioned for Jack to move farther back into the alley, and he complied.

"What do you want?" Jack asked.

"There's a powerful woman who wants you dead," Magnus replied dryly, "and I'm here to make sure that happens."

Confusion crossed the boy's face. "Why would some lady want you to kill me?"

"I can't say I understand it myself," Magnus replied. "But a contract is a contract. It's nothing personal."

This was usually the point when the target said something like "this seems *kinda* personal," but Magnus gave the boy credit for keeping that to himself. If anything, the young man stood straighter and faced his assassin with a steady gaze.

Magnus raised his blaster and fired, but instead of seeing a body slump to the ground, the smell of burnt flesh in the air, he saw the beam go wide and strike a garbage container down the alley. He fired again, but again the beam missed. This time, however, Magnus also noticed a darkened line running across Jack Groen's chest and another, similar line across his back. A whiff of smoke came off the boy's clothing where the bolt of energy had singed it.

Did he just dodge both my shots? Magnus wondered.

Before he could consider further, the boy lunged forward and rolled into a tuck before unfolding like a flower in bloom. Jack's flattened palm struck Magnus' blaster, sending it flying somewhere into the trash bins. The movement was so fast, Magnus barely saw it, but his own reaction was nearly as swift. He thrust his fist into the center of Jack's chest, sending the boy staggering backwards.

"Who trained you?" Magnus asked.

"My mother!" Jack replied and launched a flying kick through the air. This time it was Magnus' turn to dodge, leaning his body to one side as the boy sailed by.

Magnus charged, striking Jack several times before he could land and recover. The boy toppled over from the blows, but then jumped to his feet, kicking Magnus hard in the abdomen. The assassin groaned but tightened his muscles before another kick landed.

At the alley entrance, an orange general-purpose robot appeared, one of his arms hanging loosely.

"I just want to check on you--" the orange robot started, but Magnus grabbed the loose arm, tearing it from the socket in a shower of sparks. The robot turned and ran away as Magnus began hitting Jack with the mechanical arm.

The boy snatched a greasy wrench from the ground and used it to block the assassin's attacks. The metal casing of the arm dented against the heavy tool with each strike.

"Enough!" Magnus shouted, dropping the appendage while springing forward. Burying the crown of his head into the boy's sternum, Magnus sent Jack off his feet and onto his back with the killer on top of him. The wrench went spinning across the pavement.

Pinning him down, Magnus wrapped his hands around Jack's throat, his thumbs pressing into the boy's airway.

Magnus felt Jack struggling beneath him, but the killer's weight was too great.

A gurgling noise came from Jack's mouth as Magnus leaned his face closer.

"I told you," Magnus said, "it's nothing *personal*."

Watching Jack's eyes roll back into his head, Magnus saw his face turn pale.

Just let go, Magnus was thinking when something hit him fast and hard. He rolled off the top of the boy and into a garbage can, the lid clattering on the ground. Looking up, he saw a woman of Asian heritage standing over them both.

She did not look amused.

"Lucy?" Magnus asked.

Coughing and struggling to breathe, Jack got to his feet while holding his throat. Magnus stood as well. Both stared at Lefty Lucy.

"What are you doing here?" both men asked simultaneously.

Magnus and the boy looked at each other.

"You know her?" they said together.

Lucy's eyes glanced upward at the sliver of sky above the alley.

"This is Lefty Lucy," Jack said, his voice raspy.

"I'm aware of that," Magnus replied. "How do *you* know her?"

"She's my mother," Jack said. "Well, I mean she raised me..."

Magnus gave them both a hard look before realization flashed across his face.

"How old are you?" he asked Jack.

"Sixteen."

Magnus and Lucy's eyes met and he finally understood.

"I'm Magnus Black," he told the boy. "I'm the one who brought you to Lucy when you were a baby."

For a few seconds, it was Jack's turn to process what was happening, but when he did, he lunged at Magnus again, only to find Lucy between them.

"You killed my mother!" Jack shouted.

Magnus nodded. "Yes, I did."

"But why?" Jack asked.

"It was a job," Magnus replied. "It wasn't--"

"Personal," Jack said bitterly. "Yeah, I heard you the first time."

All three remained silent until Magnus spoke.

"I need you to come with me," he told the boy.

"What the hell for?" Jack asked.

"Lady Veber has a contract out on your life," Magnus explained. "We need to pay her a visit and convince her to cancel the contract."

"And what if she doesn't?" Jack said.

"I can be very convincing," Magnus replied. "Now, go pack a bag and meet me at my ship, the *Starling*, in an hour."

Lucy glared at the assassin.

"I'll take care of him," Magnus said.

Her eyes only narrowed.

"And I *promise* I won't kill him," Magnus replied.

The representatives of each of the Five Families arrived once again on Lokeren. This time, Lord Tagus III brought Burkebot to ensure someone was there to record his inevitable victory.

After freshening up, each representative entered the dining hall of the Veber estate and took their seat at the round table in the center. As before, Prince Richard sat directly across from Lady Veber. To Richard's left, Lady Olivia Montros occasionally cast her eyes in his direction but mostly stared at the rings on her fingers. To the right of the prince, Tagus and his ally, Lord Vincent Groen, were seated while Burkebot stayed out of the way in the corner of the room.

For her part, Lady Veber wasted no time opening the proceedings.

"I declare the Imperial Conclave reconvened," she said.

Tagus, who had entered the room already smiling, snickered in apparent glee.

Lady Veber rolled her eyes. "Calm down."

Tagus coughed and composed himself, but remained grinning like a boy about to open an enormous birthday present.

"Before we vote on the nominations," Lady Veber continued, "I will call them out, one by one, and have you reaffirm them.

"Lady Montros?" she asked. "Are you still content with your nomination?"

Olivia nodded.

"Lord Tagus?" Lady Veber said. "Are you as well?"

Tagus scoffed. "Of course!"

Lastly, she looked at the prince, her eyes imploring.

"And you, Prince Richard?" she asked.

"Yes," Richard replied without hesitation, drawing a collective sigh from most of the others at the table.

"Very well then," Lady Veber said with resignation in her voice. "Let us vote, starting with Lord Groen and ending with me..."

"Me?" Vincent replied. "Alright then, my vote goes to Lord Tagus."

"What a surprise!" Tagus joked, patting him on the arm. "And, to the astonishment of no one, I vote for myself *as well*."

"That means you now have two votes, Lord Tagus," Lady Veber replied, barely able to contain a groan. "If you gain *one* more vote, *you* will be the winner."

Tagus nodded at Lady Veber, his eyes trained on her face as if to say, *A deal is a deal.* Instead of returning his gaze, however, she turned to Prince Richard.

"I vote for myself," Richard said.

"And what about you, Lady Montros?" Lady Veber asked. "A vote for Tagus will give him victory. A vote for Prince Richard would give both of them two votes. Or you could--"

"I vote for myself!" Olivia said and glared at the prince.

Tagus laughed. "Good for you!"

"Then that means Prince Richard and Lady Montros have one vote apiece," Lady Veber said, "and Lord Tagus has two votes."

Tagus squirmed in his seat, ready to jump up at any moment. Lady Veber knew what he was expecting and knew what he might do if she failed to cast the winning vote in his favor.

"Go on," he said, daring her to defy him. "Correct your family's mistake. Don't let history repeat itself."

All eyes were on Lady Veber, even Burkebot's electronic ones as the robot took a few steps closer to get a better view.

She cleared her throat.

"I vote for Lady Montros," she said.

"What?" Tagus asked.

Lady Veber leaned over Vincent, getting as close to Tagus as possible.

"I will *never* vote for you," she hissed. "Not even with my *dying* breath!"

"But that means nobody has a majority..." Vincent remarked, grasping the obvious.

"Yes," Lady Veber replied, sitting back in her seat. "The Imperial Conclave is again adjourned."

The *Starling* hurled through hyperspace with Magnus Black in the cockpit. After double-checking the course, Magnus climbed down a ladder into a narrow corridor leading to the galley where Jack Groen was waiting. A table and chair, normally stowed when not in use, were folded out so Jack had a place to sit. With nowhere else to take a seat, Magnus leaned against the wall.

The boy stared at him.

"You don't have to look at me like that," Magnus said. "I already promised your mother I wouldn't hurt you."

Jack scoffed. "As if you could."

"As I recall," Magnus went on, "your lights were about to go out when Lucy came to your rescue."

"I'm not afraid of you."

"Well," Magnus said, "you *should* be."

The assassin reached over Jack and removed a ready-made meal from a dispenser in the wall. He dropped it on the table in front of the boy.

"Hungry?" Magnus asked.

Jack examined the packaged meal dubiously. "You spoil me."

"Only the best for royalty," Magnus remarked.

The boy opened the meal which began heating itself almost immediately. A pair of plastic utensils were attached along the side.

"What is it?" Jack asked.

"No idea."

The boy took a bite.

"I think it's beef," he said.

"Mystery solved," Magnus replied, turning back toward the cockpit.

"Wait," Jack said.

"What?"

"I wanted to ask you about my mother," the boy said. "I mean, my *real* mother."

Magnus raised an eyebrow. "Is that a good idea?"

"I never met her," Jack said, "and you were the last one to see her alive... before you killed her..."

"Listen, kid," Magnus said. "I already told you it was a job and nothing more than that. If I hadn't killed her, somebody else would have. Sometimes, it's just your time to die."

"But who decided that?" Jack asked. "Who wanted them dead?"

Magnus didn't answer.

Not waiting, Jack asked, "And why didn't you kill me too?"

Magnus leaned against the wall again, this time crossing his arms.

"My parents were colonists on one of the outer worlds," he began. "One day raiders landed and started killing everybody. My mother, nine months pregnant, was lined up in front of a ditch and shot, along with the other surviving settlers."

Jack's mouth opened to speak, but said nothing.

"Anyway," Magnus went on, "after the raiders left, a group of pirates came to pick over whatever was left to salvage. They found me in the pit next to my mother. Her last living act was to give birth to me, and so when I saw you lying there in your mother's dead arms, something made me stop. I just couldn't kill you."

"And you gave me to Lucy..."

"That's right."

"Do you regret it?" the boy asked.

"Saving your life?" Magnus asked. "Or being a killer?"

"Either, I guess."

"No," Magnus replied.

Jack was silent, studying the food in front of him.

"This is terrible," he said finally.

"Yeah," Magnus agreed. "It usually is."

Burkebot was named after a human, but watching Tagus III throw small furniture around his suite at the Veber estate, Burkebot could not fathom his employer's human behavior. A chair sailed across the room, striking a dresser and splintering into pieces.

"If this is an attempt to redecorate," Burkebot said, "I find it highly inefficient."

"I'll *kill* her!" Tagus shouted, scanning the room for more furniture.

"Who?" the robot asked.

With eyes wide open, Tagus faced the robot. "Lady Veber!"

"That seems unwise," Burkebot replied.

"Why not?" Tagus asked, picking an expensive vase off a table. "She killed my father!"

"True, but perhaps you should give it more thought before you do anything--"

The vase smashed against the wall.

"--rash," Burkebot finished.

"Once I'm emperor," Tagus snarled, "I'll eradicate the whole Veber family. I'll string them up and stick their heads on spikes!"

Humans, Burkebot had observed, were often irrational, letting their emotions run away with them, especially *rage*. It dominated their daily lives from the moment they read the news in the morning to when they lay down to a fitful sleep at night. Like toddlers in dire need of a timeout, humans erupted into tantrums, stomping and shouting until their tempers cooled. Their unpredictability was what bothered Burkebot the most.

It made him nervous.

"We had a deal!" Tagus said, though his heavy breathing suggested he was running out of steam.

"Did you intend to honor the deal?" Burkebot asked.

"That's beside the point..."

"Perhaps Lady Veber sensed your duplicity," the robot said, "and that's why she chose to vote against you?"

Tagus stopped.

"What are you saying?" he asked. "I have a *very* honest face!"

"Humans are constantly lying," the robot replied. "Frankly, I'm astounded *any* of you trust each other."

"I'm the head of the Tagus family! It's an outrage that someone wouldn't take my word, whether I mean to keep it or not!"

Burkebot had no need to breathe, but he felt compelled to take a breath and exhale it forcefully.

"Yes, sir," he said. "What will you do now?"

Instead of finding something else to throw, Tagus seemed to be genuinely thinking for a change.

"For one," he said finally, "I'll demand that everyone remain on Lokeren."

"Why?" the robot asked.

"We can't let the outside world know their leaders can't reach an agreement," Tagus replied. "We'll stay here until we can."

Although Burkebot was not entirely sure what his master said was feasible, it was still the most rational thing to come out of his mouth all day.

On one of the patios surrounding Lady Veber's estate, Lord Vincent Groen was watching the sunset fade on the horizon like the last embers of the day, extinguished by the turquoise sea. A glass of wine was balanced on the stone balustrade.

A pair of double doors behind Vincent swung open and Lady Olivia Montros stormed out, her red dress swinging in the ocean breeze.

"What's got *you* in a huff?" he asked with a wry grin.

"It's Richard," she said, joining him by the rail while eyeing his glass. "Do you have any more of that wine?"

Vincent handed her the glass. "We could share."

Olivia took it and downed the remainder of wine before handing it back to him.

"Well, so much for sharing..." Vincent remarked.

"I've been talking to Prince Richard nonstop since that disastrous vote," she said. "He simply won't listen to reason!"

"Still refuses to withdraw his nomination?" Vincent asked.

"What else?"

Vincent scratched the stubble on his chin, gazing at the empty wine glass.

"Of course, you *could* withdraw your *own* nomination," he said.

She scowled at him. "Absolutely not!"

"Suit yourself," Vincent went on, "personally I can't imagine why someone would want to be emperor..."

"It's my family's turn," she replied. "It's expected of me."

"But do you really *want* to be empress?"

Olivia stared at the sea and considered the question.

"*Empress Olivia* has a nice ring to it," she said finally.

"And you'd wear the crown beautifully too," Vincent replied. "However, the throne doesn't come without a price."

"Like what?"

"The constant public eye for one," he said. "And the endless criticisms of everything you do."

Olivia flashed a devilish smile.

"I'll poke out the public's eye," she said, "and execute anyone who criticizes me!"

"You're joking, I hope," Vincent replied.

"Of course!" she replied. "Probably..."

They watched the last ray of sunlight drown in the sea, the horizon turning from orange to shades of purple.

"Well, the crown is not for me," Vincent said. "I like my freedoms, thank you very much, and nobody's tried to assassinate me so far..."

"The day's not over yet," Olivia replied.

"Barely."

"I suppose you'll vote for Tagus no matter what?" she asked.

"*A vote for Tagus is a vote for Groen* is practically the family motto," he said, half mockingly. "Anyway, it's worked pretty well so far."

"Hmmm," she muttered. "Sounds more like they have you in their back pocket."

"It's warm and dry there," he replied. "You should try it sometime."

"I'd rather not..."

"But in all seriousness," Vincent said, "your family expects certain things from you and my family expects the same from me. Either way, I'm compelled to vote for Tagus."

Olivia blew a raspberry, which was the last thing Vincent expected.

"Lady Olivia!" he said. "That's hardly the behavior of our future empress!"

She rested her elbow on the balustrade and cradled her chin in the palm of her hand.

"I don't care," she said with a sigh.

"Let's go find more wine," Vincent suggested.

In her private quarters, Lady Veber was so preoccupied with thoughts of Lord Tagus III, she nearly forgot about Magnus Black until he requested clearance to land at the estate. Still, she was surprised to see Magnus so soon, but even more surprised to see the person he brought with him.

"Who is this?" Lady Veber asked, fearing that she already knew the answer.

The young man beside Magnus spoke up.

"I'm Jack Groen," he said.

"How *unexpected*," she replied, shooting Magnus a withering look.

The assassin, in his dark coat, returned her stare with cold determination.

"We need to talk," Magnus said.

"I imagine so," she said, gesturing toward a pair of couches and some comfortable chairs.

Although she was at first reluctant to make eye contact with the boy, Lady Veber was struck by his blue eyes and blond hair. He was not what she expected, not that she had expected him at all.

"You don't *look* like a Tagus," Lady Veber remarked.

"Well," Jack replied, momentarily at a loss, "it's possible I take after my mother..."

She smiled. "Perhaps that's for the best."

"I never knew her," Jack went on, "or my father."

"Yes, I suppose it's your father that's the problem," Lady Veber said. "Do you know why you're here?"

Jack's face turned serious. "You want to kill me."

Lady Veber raised an eyebrow, but nodded in agreement.

"That *was* the plan," she said, again glancing at Magnus, "but apparently the plan has changed."

"I didn't know who he was," Magnus spoke for the first time.

"You knew his name, didn't you?" Lady Veber asked.

"When I first met him, he was just a baby," Magnus said. "I didn't know his real name."

"A baby?" Lady Veber said. "What are you talking about?"

"I was there when his mother died," Magnus replied. "I was the one who *killed* her."

Lady Veber noticed the boy stare into his lap, his hair covering his eyes.

"A mission?" she asked.

"I was working for Secret Intelligence," Magnus said. "I was sent to assassinate Robert and Josephine Groen, along with their son."

"But you failed, apparently," Lady Veber said.

"I wasn't told their son was a baby," Magnus replied. "Once I realized the truth, the parents were both dead, but I managed to take the child and hide him with a friend."

"But his *real* father was still alive, was he not?" Lady Veber asked.

"I didn't know that either," Magnus said, "until now."

"So, what are you going to do?" Lady Veber asked. "Will you still honor the contract?"

Jack abruptly raised his head, turning to see Magnus' response.

"I want you to cancel it," the assassin replied.

Lady Veber took a deep breath before exhaling. "Today is just *full* of surprises."

"After I took the baby, I left the Intelligence Service," Magnus said. "Ever since, they've hounded me for leaving."

"Understandable," Lady Veber said.

"Maybe," Magnus replied, "but eventually I found out the real reason they wanted to punish me for failing the mission."

"Which was?" she asked.

"Someone very high up had ordered the hit on the Groen family," Magnus said. "Somebody who wanted not just the parents dead, but especially the *child*."

Jack leaned closer and Lady Veber couldn't help but do the same.

"It was Rupert Tagus II," Magnus said.

CHAPTER THIRTEEN

Having eliminated the leaders of the Griefer and the Cyberpunk gangs, Big G should have been happy.

He was not.

Things were not going as planned in Ashetown, and the boss of the Si-Sawat syndicate spent most of his days holed up in his office at the Fat Cat Casino.

Behind Big G's desk, pictures and scribbled notes were pinned to a cork board, lengths of string connecting the otherwise disjointed items. Big G himself was reclining in his chair, staring at the board while tossing a ball of string absentmindedly between his paws. A noise drew his attention, and the ball fell to the floor and rolled under his desk.

His enforcer, Max, had entered the room.

"What is it?" Big G asked, spinning his chair around to the front. Only then did he see that Max's arm was in a sling, a line of stitches running down his shaved shoulder. "Are you *okay*?"

"Sorry, boss," Max replied in his falsetto voice. "We got hit hard."

"Again?" Big G groaned.

"They got the warehouses by the Boneyards," Max said. "And somebody shot me."

"Did you see who did it?"

"Same as before, boss," Max replied. "They looked like mercenaries."

"Unbelievable!" Big G fumed, pounding a paw on the desk. "What's the point of killing my enemies if new ones just swoop in and take their place?"

Max shrugged. "I dunno, boss."

"That was a rhetorical question, Max," Big G replied.

"A rhe-what?"

"A question that doesn't need to be answered."

"Then why did you ask it?" Max asked.

Big G rubbed his furry face. "Good question."

"We keep losing territory," Max said. "What should we do?"

"*Another* good question," Big G replied.

Silence.

"Boss?" Max asked finally.

"I'm thinking!" Big G shouted.

Max started nervously scratching at his stitches.

"Don't do that," Big G said, pointing a claw at his enforcer. "I'll make you wear mittens..."

"Sorry, boss."

"That's okay, Max. Go watch some TV while I think of something..."

Max's ears perked up.

"There's a Blood Ball game on," Max remarked. "Want to watch it with me?"

"No way," Big G replied. "Too violent."

The Sous-Sol was largely empty except for smoke, like a fog bank rolling into shore. Behind the counter, Red the bartender puffed on a cigar while Thomas Martel nursed a whiskey across the bar. Munge sat beside the detective, his own stool barely able to carry the weight.

"Do you have to smoke in here?" Martel asked, waving at the thick air.

"I've got five reasons sayin' *yes*," Red replied, clenching his hand into a fist.

Munge stared at the bartender blankly.

"I'm talking about my fingers," Red told him. "Blockhead..."

"Munge smart," he replied.

"Yeah, you're smart like I'm handsome," the bartender said and blew a smoke ring.

At that moment, a pair of Tikarin goons entered the bar, their fur greased back between their ears. Before they could say a word, Munge let out a noise somewhere between a shout and a growl. For his part, Martel reached for the non-existent pistol in his empty holster.

The two felines looked at each other and left, the door closing behind them.

"What the hell was that?" Martel asked.

Red motioned toward the entrance with his smoldering cigar.

"Ever since Big G got rid of the Griefers," he said, "he's been sending mooks around to get protection money. *Stupid* here has been keeping them off our backs... for now."

Martel gave Munge an approving nod.

"But from what I hear," Red went on, "Big G might need somebody protecting *him*."

"What do you mean?" the detective asked.

"He and Si-Sawat have been losing territory to some Johnny-come-lately," Red replied. "They took over all the Lotus dens and I hear they've bought off the police too."

Martel felt the vibration of his datapad from inside his coat. Pulling it out, an unexpected name appeared on the screen.

"Lady Candice Woodwick?" he asked aloud, hesitating to accept the call.

Red snorted.

"Look at you!" he said. "Getting calls from high society!"

"Shut up," Martel muttered and stepped away from the bar before tapping the pad. Candy's face appeared with a smile, her brilliant blue eyes filling the screen.

"Detective Martel?" she asked.

The detective cleared his throat and then mentally chastised himself for not doing that *before* he answered.

"Lady Candice," he said. "This is a surprise."

"Why is it so dark?" Candy asked. "Are you in a cave?"

"Actually, I'm--" Martel glanced around. "--Yeah, I'm in a cave."

"How exciting!" she exclaimed. "You certainly live a remarkable life..."

"A thrill a minute," the detective replied. "What can I do for you?"

"Bless your heart," Candy said. "That's why I'm calling. I was hoping you could come to my uncle's apartment today."

"Is there a problem?"

"I'm afraid so," she replied. "Uncle Winnie's roommate, Lord Groen, has taken a turn for the worse. He found more Lotus and now he's had a relapse."

"Have you called a doctor?" Martel asked.

On the screen, Candy turned away briefly.

"Well," she said, "I'd like to keep this a private affair. The fewer people who know about it, the better..."

"I understand," Martel replied. "I can be there in a couple of hours."

Candy smiled and Martel's heart skipped a beat.

"Thank you so much!" she said. "I knew I could depend on you!"

After the screen went blank again, Martel looked up to see Red staring at him with his arms crossed.

"Blockhead," the bartender said.

Jessica Doric had developed a short temper of late, mostly because her boss, Lord Maycare, had become a pain to locate. Not one to carry a phone, he could be anywhere on the sprawling Maycare estate, and Doric was forced to go on a wild goose chase whenever she needed to find him.

"It's *his* damn institute!" she swore under her breath, referring to the Maycare Institute of Xeno Studies. Even so, Doric needed approval for certain expenditures, and Maycare kept a surprisingly tight hold on the organization's purse strings. Doric sometimes wondered if this was just an excuse to satisfy her boss' appetite for adrenaline-fueled adventure.

Or a tax write-off.

Having checked the gym, the outside terrace, and the media room, Doric strode down a long corridor with her clenched fists swinging by her side until she was just outside the study. Sticking her head through the doorway, Doric heard the distinct sound of crying.

"Hello?" she asked.

The crying stopped, followed by an unsteady "Yes?"

Doric entered the study and found Lady Candice in a chair by the window, a box of tissues beside her.

"Are you all right?" Doric asked.

"Of course!" Candy replied with false cheerfulness.

Doric came closer. Candy's nose was bright crimson and her eyes pink.

"Why were you crying?" Doric asked.

"Me?" Candy replied, trying to stuff the tissue box behind the chair cushion. When this failed miserably, the facade fell altogether, and the flood gates opened. She covered her eyes while tears ran out from under her hands.

For a moment, Doric wondered about leaving her alone. After all, Candy was not her favorite person and, in her opinion, the cause of much of Maycare's recent behavior. However, seeing someone like this melted her otherwise academic heart and she knelt beside the chair, putting her hand on Candy's knee to comfort her.

"It'll be okay," Doric said. "What's wrong?"

"I've done something terrible!" Candy replied between sobs.

"It can't be *that* bad..." Doric said.

Candy paused to collect herself, using a tissue to blow her nose.

"When I was still a girl," she began, "I always thought Lord Groen was having so much fun!"

"Your uncle's roommate?"

Candy nodded. "Radford would go to bet on the horses and sometimes he'd take me along. When I got old enough, he showed me how to place bets and pretty soon I was going on my own.

"At first," she went on, "I kept winning, and it was fun! Then, I had a losing spell, but I kept betting because I thought my luck would change. Pretty soon I was getting deeper and deeper into debt. After using all my credit, I asked Radford and he told me about someone named Jollux. Jollux was the only one willing to loan me money."

"Oh, Lady Candice..."

"I know!" Candy cried. "I'm so embarrassed!"

Through the doorway, Henry walked into the study with his hands in his pockets.

"Go away, Henry!" Doric shouted.

Henry spun on his heels and strolled back out of the room.

"So, what happened?" Doric asked.

"Jollux called me yesterday," Candy replied. "He said I needed to contact that detective, Martel, and tell him to meet me."

"Why?"

"I don't know!" Candy sobbed. "But I'm worried. Jollux is dangerous..."

"Call Martel back and warn him," Doric said.

"It's too late. He was supposed to meet me two hours ago."

"Maybe we should call the police," Doric suggested.

"They can't be trusted," Candy replied. "Jollux paid them off."

"Have you told Lord Maycare?"

Candy's eyes widened. "No! Devlin can't know about this!"

"You have to tell him."

"No!" Candy said, more determined this time. "There *has* to be another way."

From the skies above Middleton, a gravcar swooped down and landed in the driveway of a dilapidated mansion slowly being restored by laborers. The workers scarcely acknowledged the two plain-clothed detectives who exited the vehicle or the man they removed from the backseat, his hands in cuffs and his head covered with a black hood. This was not unusual at the house.

The homicide detectives, Wingus and Dingus, dragged the man up to the front door where a muscular man dressed as a butler let them in. The butler ushered them through to the hothouse where Jollux sat on his bench like on a teak throne, surrounded by tropical plants. The loan shark followed the new arrivals with his big, yellow eyes until the detectives dropped their prisoner at his feet.

Wingus pulled off the hood, revealing Thomas Martel.

"Detective Martel!" Jollux shouted. "So nice of you to join us... *again!*"

His face swollen, Martel blinked against the brightness of the room. "I didn't have a lot of choice..."

"Of course you did!" Jollux replied. "If you hadn't continued digging into my gambling racket, you wouldn't be here!"

Jollux eyed the two police detectives.

"Did you have any trouble securing our guest?" he asked them.

"He was right where you said he'd be," Wingus replied. "We brought his gun along too, in case you wanted a souvenir."

Taking a clear evidence bag out of his coat, Wingus placed it on the bench next to the loan shark.

"He calls it *Maxwell*," he said, returning to his spot beside the other detective.

"You gave your gun a name?" Jollux asked incredulously. "How peculiar..."

Finding it hard to keep his head up, Martel stared at the floor. "It takes all kinds, I guess."

"Oh, I agree with you there," the loan shark said. "I see all sorts in my line of business, from gutter urchins to ladies of high society. Speaking of which, I believe we share an acquaintance, Lady Candice Woodwick, do we not?"

"Yeah," Martel muttered.

"You realize, of course, she was the one who set you up."

Though it hurt his jaw to smile, the detective grinned sardonically.

"I kinda figured that when these two morons showed up," he said. "But I was hoping it was just a coincidence."

"Sadly, no," Jollux replied. "In fact, Lady Candice owes me quite a lot of money so she was eager to make things right, and not for the *first* time I might add."

Dingus, who had been holding Martel by the arm this whole time, let go, allowing the detective to fall to his knees.

"Uncuff the poor man," Jollux said. "Assuming you've searched him, of course."

Unable to stand after the detectives removed his shackles, Martel fell face first. Wingus and Dingus picked him up again, but Martel was now holding something, a snub pistol that had been stashed away in his waistband.

"Say hello to *Mini Max*," Martel said, firing into the top of Wingus' shoe before doing the same thing to Dingus. Both men released their hold on Martel while they hopped around, blood spurting from their respective feet.

Martel pointed the pistol at Jollux, but the weight of the butler landed on him with full force, flattening the detective. The muscular goon wrestled the gun from Martel's weakened hands.

Wingus fell, unable to balance on one foot while trying to stem the blood spilling from the other. Lying on his side, he pointed at the now subdued investigator. "Kill him!"

Jollux rested his arms thoughtfully on his Buddha belly.

"Perhaps you're right," he sighed, nodding at his butler still atop the detective. "As I recall, our friend still deserves payback for demolishing one of my Lotus dens. It seems only fitting that he gets a taste of what so many others have already tried..."

The butler nodded and pulled a handful of Lotus tabs from his pocket. Forcing Martel's mouth open, he shoved the petals inside while clamping the detective's nose shut. Unable to breathe, Martel choked until he swallowed what was in his mouth.

"Pleasant dreams..." Jollux chuckled.

The mean streets of Regalis, and the Ashetown district in particular, were a tough place for a rookie, but Police Detective Thomas Martel wasn't a rookie anymore and hadn't been for a long time. After years under his partner Detective Crawley's guidance, Martel believed he had already made all the choices required to shape him into an officer and a person.

He was wrong.

Their gravcar landed beside the crumbling facade of an abandoned apartment building in an Ashetown neighborhood. Before they got out, Crawley handed Martel a credit stick.

"What's this for?" Martel asked.

"Just hold on to it for a while," Crawley growled, his breath reeking of cigarette smoke.

With Martel close behind, Crawley went inside and climbed the stairs until they came out onto the fourth floor. The hallways were empty except for rodents and trash left behind by squatters. When they reached one of the apartments, Crawley unlocked the door and walked in. When Martel followed, he saw a man cuffed to a metal chair in the otherwise empty room. The man's head hung as if sleeping.

Martel recognized the uniform and the badge. His name tag read *Ledetchko*.

"He's a cop," Martel said.

Crawley flashed a sarcastic grin. "Nothing gets by you, kid."

The senior detective slapped the man awake.

"Let me go," Ledetchko moaned.

"I'd love to," Crawley replied, "but we have some unfinished business."

"I already said *no*," the officer told him.

"Yeah, but I'm giving you a second chance," Crawley said. "I've got a big heart. The doctor says it's because of the drinkin', but I'd like to think it's because I'm a reasonable man."

Crawley removed the cuffs. As the policeman raised his head, Martel saw his face was swollen and bruised.

"This is my partner, Martel," Crawley said.

"Is he as dirty as you?" Ledetchko asked, which earned him a quick slap from the senior detective.

"Don't be rude," Crawley said. "Martel brought you a gift..."

Martel knew what came next. He took the credit stick out of his pocket and brought it over to the chair. The officer scowled at him.

"Big G would like you to accept this offering of his gratitude," Crawley told the officer. "Consider it your reward for being part of something greater than yourself."

Martel stood in front of the officer, the credit stick no bigger than a thumb drive.

"No," Ledetchko said. "I told you, I'm not taking any bribes!"

"Since you're new to the department," Crawley said, "I'll explain how things work. You see, a system like ours is based on trust. Without trust, the system breaks down. If we all take the bribe, we know each of us has a vested interest in watching each other's backs. United we stand, divided we fall."

"Screw you, Crawley!" the officer shouted.

The senior detective put his hands on Ledetchko's face, pressing the officer's cheeks together.

"We can't have a rookie like you mucking things up by staying *clean*," Crawley continued. "If you don't take the bribe, we can't trust you and the system breaks down. That's no good for anybody."

Releasing his hold on the officer, Crawley took out a pistol. Just by looking at it, Martel could tell it was a ghost gun, a 3D-printed pistol without markings and nearly impossible to trace.

"Are you going to shoot me?" Ledetchko asked.

"No," Crawley replied, offering the weapon to Martel. "*He* is."

Martel recoiled, taking a step away from his partner's outstretched hand.

"Crawley..." he said.

"In for a penny, in for a pound," his partner said. "It has to be done by somebody, so why not you?"

"I..." Martel stammered.

"Come on now," Crawley replied, his voice growing firmer. "It's about trust. How can I trust a man who won't back up his partner?"

Putting away the credit stick, Martel took the ghost gun from his partner.

"You don't have to do this," Ledetchko said. "I've heard about you, Martel. I know you're not like Crawley. If you do this, you'll be no better than him."

"Go ahead," Crawley told Martel. "Do what's *right*."

Martel's finger curled around the trigger, the grip of the handle pressed against Martel's skin.

"I have a family," Ledetchko said, his voice starting to quiver.

Martel looked pleadingly at his partner, but Crawley's eyes stared back with nothing but cruelty.

"Do it," Crawley said.

Martel fired three shots into the officer's chest. Ledetchko's body convulsed before going limp, his head hanging down like it was when they first entered the room.

The pistol, its molecular structure activated by the heat of being fired, began to dissolve in Martel's hand. Within moments, the gun had transformed into granules, pouring through Martel's fingers like sand.

Munge had been using a lint roller unsuccessfully when a woman walked into the bar asking for help. Munge attempted to think of an accompanying joke, but was just as unsuccessful as the lint roller.

"Who are you?" Red asked from behind the bar.

"I'm Lady Candice Woodwick," the woman said. "I'm afraid Detective Martel is in terrible danger and his secretary told me someone here might be able to help."

"You're that society dame that Martel went to meet," Red replied, crossing his meaty arms. "I *knew* it was a trap..."

"I'm sorry," Candy said. "It was all a big mistake, but I'm hoping it's not too late."

"Do you know where he is?" Red asked.

"I think so," she replied.

Munge laid the lint roller on the bar and stood up from his stool, towering over the young woman.

"Munge help," he said.

After getting the address from Candy, Munge arrived shortly after sunset at the mansion where Martel was allegedly being held. The workers had gone home for the day and the grounds were quiet except for the occasional guard who Munge pummeled into unconsciousness. In the twilight, the glass dome of the hothouse glowed like a diamond. Taking a length of pipe from one of the scaffolds, Munge smashed through the dome's shell and came face to face with the frog-like creature Candy had called *Jollux*.

"Where Martel?" Munge demanded, holding the pipe menacingly in his hand.

Jollux raised his spindly arms, his giant eyes like black disks. "I've no idea what you mean!"

A butler with the physique of a bodybuilder rushed into the hothouse brandishing a large pistol. Munge had seen the gun before.

"Why you have Maxwell?" he asked.

"Put the pipe down!" the butler replied.

"Okay," Munge said, but instead of dropping the pipe, he flung it across the room, striking the butler in the arm. Maxwell fell to the floor with a heavy *thud*.

Munge descended on the butler with surprising speed, shoving him like a doll into some orchids. Jollux let out a cry as if someone had landed on his children.

Taking the pistol from the ground, Munge pointed the weapon at the loan shark.

"Munge ask again," he said. "*Where Martel?*"

CHAPTER FOURTEEN

Several weeks ago, Lady Candice was standing in the blustery, arctic wind. She had never been to a hypersled race before, let alone at the south pole of the planet Aldorus, but she had dressed warmly in a pink down coat and leather gloves.

With the VIP pass that her boyfriend, Lord Devlin Maycare, had given her, Candy made her way down to the staging area where the hypersleds were kept just before being moved onto the track. Now shielded from the wind, Candy could smell the rocket fuel that permeated the air.

"Candy!" a deep, manly voice shouted. "Over here!"

Pulling down her hood, Candy saw Maycare waving. He wore a blue racing suit with a silver stripe running down the side. Candy waved back and made her way through the other track personnel until she found herself in Maycare's arms.

I hope he doesn't get oil on my new coat! she thought.

"You made it!" Maycare said, relaxing his hug.

"I wouldn't miss it for the world!" she replied. "It's so exciting!"

Maycare grinned broadly and gestured toward the sled beside him.

"Let me introduce you to the *Number 9*," he said.

To Candy's untrained eye, the sled was little more than a canopy with rockets, all bolted precariously to skis.

"Is it safe?" she asked.

"More or less," Maycare replied.

"Well," Candy replied, "I assume you know what you're doing."

From the surrounding crowd, a robot appeared with a datapad tucked under his arm.

"You remember my butlerbot, Benson?" Maycare asked.

"Yes, of course," Candy said. "How are you, Benson?"

"Very well, Lady Candice," the robot replied. "I was wondering if I could borrow Lord Maycare for a moment?"

"What do you need?" Maycare asked.

"I wanted to give you my report on Lord Grayson's sled, sir," Benson said, holding out the datapad.

Maycare shook his fist. "My nemesis!"

"Indeed, sir," Benson replied drolly.

"Sorry, my dear," Maycare told Candy. "It won't be a minute..."

Her eyelashes fluttering, Candy smiled. "Of course, darling."

While Maycare and his butlerbot consulted, engulfed by the ebb and flow of the crowd, Candy drew closer to the Number 9, her hands in her coat pockets. She felt her heart pounding as she remembered what Jollux had told her.

In his hothouse, the loan shark had held a small box in his bony fingers.

"What's this?" Candy had asked.

"Just a device," Jollux replied. "Consider it a little present for Lord Maycare."

"What does it do?" Candy said, taking the box.

"Hopefully, it will explode."

Candy shrank back before Jollux calmed her.

"Don't worry, Lady Candice," he said. "Just a little boom, that's all. Just enough to damage the engine around it."

"What engine?" Candy replied, staring at the box. "What in the heavens are you talking about?"

Jollux's giant eyes blinked slowly.

"I've backed several bets of late concerning a hypersled race occurring this weekend," he said. "The prevailing wisdom thinks your boyfriend, Lord Maycare, will win. This will make sure he doesn't, and make several people indebted to me in the process."

"Like me?" Candy asked.

"Indeed," Jollux replied, "and if you wish me to forgive some of your debts, you'll do what I say."

Standing beside the blue and silver Number 9, Candy held the box in her hands. She glanced as casually as possible to the right and left, but the other racers and crews were preoccupied with their own business rather than paying attention to her. Even Maycare and Benson were engrossed in conversation, ignoring Candy entirely.

Taking the opportunity, she slipped the box into a nest of wires along the main body of the sled's rocket engine. When she felt a magnet on the box attach to something, she pulled her hand away.

Jollux said Devlin will eject when it explodes, Candy told herself. *I'm sure he'll be alright...*

Maycare returned and gave her another hug.

"Are you ready?" he asked, releasing her again.

Candy smiled back, but secretly wanted to cry.

Although it was technically Benson's job, Henry brought a glass of water for Lady Candice. She was standing watch over Thomas Martel as he lay in a coma in one of the bedrooms on the Maycare estate. A heart monitor and other medical devices stood beside the bed like totems while Martel slept, and a nursebot remained nearby, rented by Maycare from YouSickWeFix Medical Supplies and Services.

Henry took the water over to the chair where Candy sat.

"Oh, thank you, Henry," she said. "Thank you for thinking of me."

Henry's cheeks flushed red. "It's no trouble! How is Mister Martel?"

"There's no change, I'm afraid," she remarked, her eyes turning back on Martel.

"Shouldn't he be in a hospital or something?" Henry asked.

"This is safer," Candy replied. "Who knows who else might try to kill him!"

Henry, adjusting his feet awkwardly, spied the brushed chrome of Maxwell on the nightstand. He took a step toward it.

"Don't touch that," Doric's voice said sternly from the doorway.

Henry stopped.

"I wasn't--" he began.

"Just *don't*," Doric said, coming into the room.

"Hello, Jessica dear," Candy said, her voice sweet in contrast. "Checking up on our patient?"

"Just keeping an eye on *this* one," she replied, nodding toward Henry.

"I thought Candy might be thirsty," he said innocently.

"Uh huh," Doric replied.

"Candy said Martel hasn't changed," he went on.

"Well, he's in a coma," Doric said.

"He might come out of it," Henry said.

Doric looked doubtfully at the detective's near-lifeless body.

"I suppose," she said. "Nobody knows much about Lotus."

Someone else appeared in the doorway. This time it was Benson the butlerbot, carrying a small box.

"What is it?" Doric asked.

"A package was just delivered," the robot replied. "It's addressed to Detective Martel."

Candy's eyes widened in alarm. "Who knows he's even here?"

"It also came with this note," Benson said, handing both to Doric. She read the note aloud.

"For Martel," she said, "from a *friend*."

"What if it's a bomb?" Henry remarked.

"I already scanned the package," Benson replied. "There's no evidence of an explosive but there is indeed a device inside. Would you like me to open it instead?"

"That won't be necessary," Doric said, breaking the seal of tape and pulling the cardboard flaps open.

Henry winced but, noticing nothing had exploded, immediately came closer to peer inside the box. Among some packing peanuts was an object, almost like a pistol but with a short nozzle instead of a barrel, made from white plastic.

"A gun?" he asked.

"It's a hypo-injector," Doric said, removing it from the box. She studied the side of the handle where an indicator showed the number 1. "But it only has one dose..."

"A dose of what?" Candy asked.

"I've no idea," Doric replied.

"We could take it to a lab," Henry suggested.

Doric nodded. "But that might use up the only dose."

"I'm afraid there wasn't a return address," Benson added. "Or any other indicator of who might have sent it."

"The note says it's for Detective Martel," Candy said. "I think we should give it to him."

"Sounds risky," Doric said. "Not that he has much to lose..."

"I think we should do what Candy says," Henry said.

Doric gave her assistant a dark look. "*Of course* you do."

Candy got up and, taking the injector from Doric, brought it over to the bed.

"If it's the wrong thing to do," she said, "I'll be the one responsible. You can just add it to my list."

She pressed the nozzle against Martel's arm and pulled the injector's trigger. While they waited to see what would happen next, Henry had a thought.

"You have a list?" he asked.

A few days had passed since the last vote of the Imperial Conclave. Lady Veber had used that time to record the testimony of Magnus Black and run a paternity test on Jack Groen, all of which was kept secret from the other members of the Five Families. Confident that what Magnus had said was true, Lady Veber put Jack under her own personal protection, allowing the assassin to depart.

Lady Veber watched while the dark form of the *Starling* lifted from the landing pad and rose steadily through the azure sky. Truth be told, she was eager to see him go. Although Magnus had been the one who killed Lord Tagus II, Lady Veber was the one who had hired him, and she did not need Magnus as a constant reminder of her sins.

With Magnus gone, Lady Veber went looking for Jack and found him down on the beach, his pants rolled up and his feet wading in the surf. She approached him across the hot sand, her light, blue dress twirling in the wind.

"Mister Black just left," she said. "Didn't you want to say goodbye?"

"Not really," Jack replied. "He's not exactly a *friend*."

"I suppose not," Lady Veber said. "Deep down inside, I think he'd rather kill us all..."

Jack flashed a boyish grin. "Only if someone was *paying* him."

"On the other hand," she added, "I think your half-brother Rupert would do it for free."

"It's strange to think I have a brother," Jack remarked.

"Well, I'd lower my expectations if I were you."

Jack nodded.

"I saw him in the news while I was growing up," he said. "I know the things he's done."

"The media only tells what they know," Lady Veber replied. "There's a great many things they know nothing about."

Jack splashed his feet in the water.

"You know I've never been on another planet before," he said.

"Really?"

"Actually," he corrected himself, "I was on my parent's planet Galanis when I was a baby. The one where they died..."

"Perhaps it's best you don't remember," Lady Veber replied.

"I guess so."

"You know I had a son once," she went on. "He used to play on this beach when he was a boy."

"What was he like?" Jack asked.

"A lot like his father," she replied. "I miss them..."

Jack watched the ripples around his feet. "I'm sorry."

"The past is gone," Lady Veber said, "even if it revisits us from time to time."

From the estate, two figures appeared, each wearing swimming attire. Lady Olivia Montros was dressed in a red one-piece while Lord Vincent Groen wore trunks and had a beach ball under one arm and a towel draped over his shoulder. Seeing the others, Vincent shouted across the beach, "A little overdressed, don't you think?"

Jack and Lady Veber exchanged looks and laughed.

"Come over here!" Lady Veber shouted back. "I want you to meet someone!"

When Martel woke up, he was a lot less dead than he had been expecting. Seeing the crowd of people around his bed was also a surprise. Lady Candice, Jessica Doric, Henry Riff, and the butlerbot were all staring at him expectantly. A nursebot, however, stayed largely indifferent behind them.

"Am I late to the party?" he said.

"You've been in a coma," Doric replied.

Martel became slowly aware of the IV running from the back of his hand and the steady rhythm of a heart monitor beeping nearby. It wasn't the first time he had been in a hospital bed, but this was by far the nicest hospital he had ever seen.

"Where am I?" he asked.

"You're the guest of Lord Maycare at his estate," Benson said. "Please make yourself at home."

"It looks like I already have," Martel replied.

"What do you remember?" Doric asked.

Martel took a second or two, but the memories slowly emerged from his foggy mind. "I remember somebody shoving a bunch of Lotus in my mouth. Can't say it tasted good..."

"You overdosed," Doric said. "We thought you might never wake up."

"Well, I'm awake now," Martel replied, "unless this is another dream."

"It's not," Doric said. "Lady Candice and Mister Munge rescued you and brought you here."

Candy finally spoke, "It was really all Munge's doing."

Martel's eyes fell on her as if seeing her for the first time. "Was it?"

Candy's face flared crimson. "Yes."

"They got your gun back too!" Henry exclaimed, pointing helpfully at the nightstand where Maxwell lay like a polished cannon.

Martel sat up in bed. "I guess the band's back together..."

"We should let him rest," Doric said. "Come on, Henry."

Visibly disappointed, Henry obeyed and, along with the others, headed toward the door.

"Lady Candice," Martel said, "if you don't mind, I'd like you to stay."

Candy stopped in her tracks while the others left more rapidly than before. Henry took a last look at her before closing the door behind him. Cautiously, she came closer to the bed.

"Yes?" she said.

"I guess I should thank you for telling Munge where I was," Martel said.

Candy smiled. "Yes."

"Although I wouldn't have been there if you hadn't set me up," he finished.

Candy's smile disappeared. "Yes."

"How much do you owe Jollux?" the detective asked.

"Too much," she replied, her eyes refusing to meet Martel's. "With interest, I could never pay it off on my own."

"So, he asked you for a favor?"

"He asked, but it's clear I had no choice. He could ruin me..."

Martel's brown eyes grew dark.

"Those men were going to kill me," he said. "A pretty big price for the value of your reputation."

"I know!" Candy said. "I was so worried! That's when I went to your office and talked to Dolores. She's the one who said Mister Munge could help."

"Well, remind me to give him a raise after Lord Maycare pays me," Martel replied. "You know your boyfriend hired me to find out who sabotaged his racing sled."

Candy's complexion, which had been bright red, now drained away, becoming as pale as the sheets covering Martel's bed.

"I know it was you, Lady Candice," Martel went on. "The only question is which one of us is going to tell Maycare."

"He'll leave me," Candy said.

"Probably," Martel replied. "Wouldn't you?"

Candy started crying.

"Yes," she answered. "I'm a terrible person!"

Martel steeled his heart, but seeing her tears made him regret being harsh.

"Listen," he said, "I've done a lot of awful things. Things that haunt my nightmares and things I may never atone for, but you can't change the past. All you can do is be a better person and hope it evens out somehow."

Candy glanced up. "Do you really believe that?"

Now it was Martel's turn to look away.

"Yeah," he said. "I have to..."

After the last unsuccessful vote of the Imperial Conclave, Lord Tagus III had demanded all representatives of the Five Families remain on Lokeren, and for once Prince Richard agreed with him. During that time, the prince stayed mostly in his quarters, the furnishings and amenities even more luxurious than Lady Veber's, reflecting Richard's status as the son of the emperor.

He lingered in the living room while the nurse finished feeding his son, Mason, in a side chamber. When she emerged, the nurse handed the baby, wrapped in swaddling clothes, to the prince who quickly sent her away so he could be alone with his boy. In the rich light coming through the window, Mason's face had the same judgmental gaze as his mother.

"It's all right," the prince said. "We'll be headed home soon enough."

A few hours later, Prince Richard entered the great hall where the conclave was taking place. The round table in the middle elicited both excitement and a sense of dread in his mind. The members of the conclave had voted twice now without a resolution, and the prince was not hopeful today would be any different.

Shortly after the prince took his place at the table, Lord Tagus arrived as well, although without Lord Groen in tow. Both men exchanged scowls before ignoring each other entirely for several minutes.

"Where are those imbeciles?" Tagus remarked finally.

"I was wondering why Vincent didn't show up with you," Richard replied. "Was he done licking your boots?"

Tagus snickered at the thought before collecting himself.

"He's probably chasing after Olivia," he said. "He has no chance, you know. She's obviously out of his league..."

"True," the prince said.

At that moment, both Lady Olivia Montros and Lord Vincent Groen entered the hall together. Lady Veber followed them moments later and ordered the doors shut.

After everyone had sat down, Lady Veber brought the proceedings to order.

"I have once again assembled the conclave," she said, "so we can have another vote."

"Unless you're going to pull a rabbit out of your hat," Tagus sneered, "we're just wasting our time."

"As a matter of fact," Lady Veber said, "I *do* have something new to share."

"Really?" Prince Richard asked.

"Assuming the original nominations still stand..." she continued while noting the nods around the table, "I would like to nominate someone as well."

"You do?" Tagus and Richard replied simultaneously.

Lady Veber drew herself up in her chair and took a long breath.

"I nominate Jack Groen," she said.

Tagus and the prince looked at each other as if to say *Who?*

The main doors opened and a young man with blond hair and blue eyes, still in his teens, entered and approached the table. He looked both surprised and a bit bewildered.

"Who the devil is this?" Tagus growled.

"In fairness," Lady Veber said, "although his last name is Groen, by blood he is actually from the House of Tagus."

"The hell he is!" Tagus shouted. "I've never seen him in my life!"

"Nevertheless," Lady Veber went on, "he *is* your father's son and your half-brother."

Tagus stood up and, as was his habit, slammed his fists on the table. "This is an *outrage!*"

"To be honest," Prince Richard said, "I agree. Traditionally, no one would think to nominate a half-blood to be emperor."

"Traditionally," Lady Veber replied, "a member of the sitting emperor's family does not nominate himself, *either.*"

The prince gave Lady Veber a foul glare, nearly matching the one Tagus was giving her.

"What proof do you have that this boy is my relation?" Tagus asked.

Lady Veber motioned to her servants who placed datapads in front of each person at the table.

"As you can see," she said, "a paternity test and a DNA scan all confirm that Jack Groen is the son of Lord Tagus II."

She then added, "By way of Lord Robert Groen's wife, Lady Josephine."

"That's a lie!" Tagus shouted, his face bright red. "He would never--"

"He did," Vincent finally spoke. "I hate to say it, but it's true."

Deflated, Tagus paused to catch his breath and sat back in his chair. "I don't believe it."

"Regardless," Lady Veber said, "we will now vote on the nominations."

"I think we should postpone for the time being," Prince Richard suggested.

"I disagree," she replied, "and as the head of these proceedings, I will cast my vote first." Gesturing for Jack to come forward, Lady Veber put her hand on his arm. "I vote for Jack Groen."

"So be it," the prince replied grimly. "I vote for myself."

"This is madness!" Tagus roared.

"What is your vote?" Lady Veber asked.

"Myself obviously!" Tagus said, turning to Vincent Groen beside him. "And the Groen family will vote for me as well."

"No," Vincent replied. "We will not."

"What?" Tagus asked.

"I watched the testimony of the man who killed my aunt and uncle," Vincent began. "Your father ordered them killed to keep his misdeed a secret. He even wanted his own baby murdered. It wasn't enough that your house keeps my family under their thumb. You had to murder us too!"

Tagus, his mouth slightly ajar, was speechless for the first time in his life.

"I *also* vote for Jack Groen," Vincent said.

Lady Veber went on, "There is only one more vote to be cast."

All eyes, including those of Jack Groen, fell on Olivia Montros. In her red dress, she returned their stares with an air of arrogance.

"I deserve to be empress," she said proudly. "It was my family's turn after all." She flashed a mischievous grin at Vincent who smiled back. "Still, I like the thought of a Groen on the throne, even if he's really a Tagus...

"I vote for Jack Groen," she said.

"With three votes," Lady Veber said, "Jack Groen has been elected by the Imperial Conclave. He will be the next emperor of the Imperium!"

CHAPTER FIFTEEN

A few days had passed, and Thomas Martel felt he was well enough to leave the Maycare estate. Mostly, however, he just wanted a drink at the Sous-Sol. A gravtaxi later, he was descending the steps and pushing open the door to his favorite dive bar.

Red, seeing Martel come in, appeared unaware the detective had been gone.

"Did you hear the news?" the bartender asked gruffly.

Martel mounted a bar stool. "I've been in a coma..."

"They elected a new emperor," Red went on, pouring a whiskey. "Some kid, apparently."

Martel accepted the glass Red offered and took a drink.

"Good for him," Martel replied.

Red refilled the glass.

"Hey," he said, "are you still going to jail for killing that Irishman?"

"I already told you I didn't kill him," Martel said with a scowl. "Anyway, all the charges were dropped."

"Good to have friends in high places, I guess," Red replied.

Martel raised the glass. "Yeah."

"Oh right, I think Louis wants to talk to you."

Getting up, Martel wasn't sure if the wobbliness in his legs was due to the whiskey or the coma. He steadied himself against the bar and came around to Red's side before knocking on the door to Louis' office.

"*Entrez,*" a voice said.

As soon as the door cracked open, the heavy odor of fish assaulted Martel's nose.

"It smells like a fish market in here--" he started.

Louis wore rubber boots and waders with suspenders pulled over a thick turtleneck sweater, along with a red wool cap. Since Louis lacked visible ears, a pair of wire-frame glasses was taped to the side of his face.

"The sea, once it casts its spell," he said in a heavy accent, "holds one in its net of wonder forever."

"What?" Martel asked.

"People attack the sea," Louis replied. "I make *love* to it."

"What do you *want*, Louis?"

The bar owner rolled up the sea chart that had been lying on his desk and gave Martel a thoughtful look.

"I worried *pour vous,*" Louis said.

"Worried about what?"

"*You*, Monsieur Martel."

"I'm fine," Martel replied.

"I can't help but feel -- how do you say -- *responsable* for sending you to Monsieur Kid."

"I don't think that's how you say it," Martel replied, "but I don't think you're to blame. A lot happened after I saw Kid."

"*Bon*," Louis said. "And this business with the Lotus?"

"The news says Warlock Industries came up with an antidote," Martel replied. "The government is handing it out to the addicts."

"An antidote, you say? How *à propos...*"

"Yeah," Martel said, his brows creasing. "It was, wasn't it?"

"So you *do* know French, *mon ami*!" Louis replied, his eyes widening until one of the earpieces came unstuck.

Martel scratched the back of his head. "Maybe a little."

Lord Maycare was speaking to someone on his datapad when Jessica Doric entered the media room. Seeing her, Maycare signaled for Doric to stay until his call was over. The face of a man wearing a panama hat appeared on the datapad's screen.

"I don't know what to tell you, Ducky," Maycare said.

"But Devlin," Ducky replied, "I've been banned from the country club and they won't let me into Mudderfield Downs!"

"You were selling chems--" Maycare started.

"I wasn't *selling* chems!" Ducky protested. "I was *giving* them *away*!"

"Well..."

"My masseur at Zahmetli Hamami gave me an even rougher massage than usual and told me never to come back!" Ducky said. "I think he might have broken one of my ribs!"

"Did you sell him Lotus?" Maycare asked.

"No, but I *gave* him a great deal..."

"There's really nothing I can do, Ducky," Maycare replied.

"But I've run out of Lotus and I can't get any more!" Ducky said. "I haven't slept in days!"

Maycare's expression softened.

"I'm sorry about that," he said. "There's an antidote apparently. Maybe that would help?"

"I don't want the antidote, Devlin," Ducky said. "I want *Lotus*!"

"I'm sorry," Maycare replied. "I can't help you."

While Maycare ended the call, Doric noticed something protruding from under a couch cushion. She gave it a pull and found herself holding a pennant for the Boneyard Bruisers.

"I guess Candy will want this back?" she wondered aloud.

"Blood ball," he replied. "What an awful sport."

"You seemed to enjoy it," Doric said.

"Only when I was watching it with Candy," Maycare replied. "Something about the blood lust in her eyes..."

Doric dropped the pennant on the couch. "So, the two of you are officially over?"

"That's right," Maycare said, glancing at the datapad still in his hands. "You know, Jess, I'm beginning to think some of my friends aren't what they seem to be."

Doric made a visible effort not to say *I told you so.*

"Yeah," she replied instead.

"But, if anything," Maycare went on, "I've learned who my real friends are."

Doric felt her cheeks redden. "Thanks."

"Through all of this, Henry has been a constant rock of support," Maycare said without irony.

"What?"

"Sometimes I don't know what I would do without him."

"Henry *Riff?*"

"Yes, of course," Maycare replied. "In fact, give him a raise. He's your subordinate, isn't he? You should really be on top of this, Jess..."

"But--"

"Just put the paperwork on my desk."

"You don't have a desk," Doric said.

"I have a study, don't I?" he asked. "I'm sure there must be a desk in there somewhere... You know, Jess, sometimes I just don't think you're paying attention."

Doric began taking deep breaths while clenching her fists.

"Yes, sir," she said calmly, and left the room.

When Prince Richard arrived at the Imperial Palace after returning to the planet Aldorus, he was met by an army of servicebots carrying crates. Like worker ants, the robots moved containers down the corridors to gravtrucks waiting at the palace entrance. The prince narrowly avoided getting squished between a crate and the doorway as he went inside the emperor's private residence. There he found his father, wearing only a robe, pointing at items he wished packed up.

"Over there," the Emperor said. "Yes, that one too..."

"You didn't waste any time," Prince Richard remarked.

"No time like the present!" his father replied cheerfully.

"You realize some of this furniture comes with the palace," Richard said, seeing an antique armchair being hauled away. "It's not *yours* to take."

Hands on hips, the emperor let his robe slip open, allowing Richard to see more than he would have liked. "Nobody's going to miss a few chairs."

"And here I thought you'd be upset with the conclave's vote," Richard said, standing to one side so a servicebot could pass by.

"Not a bit! I'd say it went better than expected..."

"A child emperor is your idea of a good thing?" Richard asked.

"He won't be ruling alone," the emperor replied. "I've already appointed Lady Veber as Imperial Regent. She'll advise him until the boy turns eighteen."

"I wasn't aware of that," Richard admitted. "Do you think that's a good idea?"

"It's better than what *you* had in mind."

The prince frowned. "I did what I thought was right."

"Don't we all, my boy!" his father said with a chuckle. "Don't we all!"

"Either way, I don't trust Lady Veber."

"Rebecca?" the emperor replied. "She's dependable and intelligent, *and* she killed a Tagus so she can't be *all* bad..."

"You really think Lord Tagus will accept the conclave vote, especially after you made his father's killer the regent?"

The emperor blew a raspberry, drawing a disapproving look from the prince.

"He hardly has a choice," the emperor replied. "Especially with the Groen family backing the decision. As far as I'm concerned, that boy Jack has more solid backing than I ever did, or most of my predecessors for that matter."

Richard nodded. "I suppose that's true."

"Of course it is!" the emperor bellowed. "Anyway, how's my grandson?"

"Good."

"Glad to hear it! I plan on spoiling him rotten!"

"Well, I just wish Lilith was still alive to see him grow up," Richard said.

"True," the emperor replied. "You were always such a good boy yourself... and a good son."

Taken aback, Richard was struck silent for a moment.

"Thank you," he said finally.

"Think nothing of it!" his father said. "Now, try to be useful and grab the end of this sofa."

Eyeing the couch doubtfully, the prince asked, "Is it yours?"

"It is now!" his father replied.

Inside the Embassy Hotel in the West End, Lord Winsor Woodwick and Lord Radford Groen were eating brunch at the Grove restaurant. Thanks to the Groen family's newfound celebrity status, the two men had been seated on the raised tier overlooking the other patrons. Complimentary mimosas in fluted glasses sat on the table.

"I say, Radford," Woodwick remarked, taking a sip from his drink, "you haven't touched your eggs Florentine."

Groen, a betting sheet for Mudderfield Downs spread out in front of him, didn't bother looking up.

"It has spinach in it," he complained.

"It's a positively divine Hollandaise sauce," Woodwick went on. "You should really try it, old man."

"Humph."

"Well, you're a grumpy goose this morning," Woodwick said. "Still suffering the after-effects of that Lotus business?"

Peering over the sheet, Groen shook his head. "No, that antidote injection did the trick."

"What is it then?"

"People keep staring at me," Groen replied, gesturing toward the various eyes cast in his direction.

"I should think so," Woodwick said. "The next emperor is a Groen after all!"

"Groen in *name* only."

"Humbug," Woodwick said, his mustache twitching. "He's your nephew! You should be quite chuffed."

"I could do without all the attention," Groen said. "Anyway, how is *your* niece these days?"

"Dreadful, I'm afraid," Woodwick said. "Candy's been heartbroken since Devlin broke it off with her."

"Can you blame him?" Groen asked.

From his overly stuffed belly, Woodwick exhaled. "No, I blame *you* for it!"

"Me?"

"Of course!" Woodwick replied. "You know jolly well you're the one who took her to the horse track."

"She said she liked horses!" Groen replied.

"But that doesn't mean she had to bet on them!"

"Well, I can't be responsible for *everything*."

"Thank heavens you didn't give her those Lotus petals."

"No, of course not!" Groen replied.

"Not that you seemed willing to share..."

"That's over and done with," Groen said. "Last I heard you can't get them anymore even if you wanted to. The supply has completely dried up..."

"Strange that, don't you think?"

Groen turned his attention back to the betting sheet without answering.

Woodwick waited until his patience wore thin. "I say, Radford, are you going to finish your eggs or not?"

"No!"

Woodwick leaned over the table and grabbed Groen's plate. With a silver fork, he dug into the eggs Florentine, yellow sauce dripping from his walrus mustache.

"Delicious!" he said.

Outside of Jollux's mansion, the sound of gunshots and blaster fire rattled the metal scaffolding, now empty of the workers who had been refurbishing the old house. Although the laborers had grown accustomed to the shady comings and goings on the mansion grounds, the fighting in the nearby neighborhood had grown too close for the workers to bear.

Like sleet, bullets sprayed the dome in the backyard, cracking the glass and sending shards falling into the hothouse. Jollux used a palm frond to shield himself from the debris.

"What's happening?" he cried helplessly.

"Big G's forces are closing in," his burly butler replied. "There's Si-Sawat goons all over the place!"

"But what about my mercenaries?" Jollux asked.

"Gone."

"What do you mean?"

"They left!" the butler said.

"But we had a deal!" Jollux shouted. "What about those two police detectives?"

"They haven't returned my calls since Martel shot them."

"Cowards," Jollux remarked. "Try reaching them again. I'm not paying those idiots to ignore me!"

The muscular butler departed, followed almost immediately by the rapid fire of a gun from the same corridor. Nearly falling off his bench, Jollux stared down the dark hallway. Out of the gloom, a Tikarin with orange fur strolled casually into the hothouse, resting a submachine gun on his hefty belly. Another gangster, his left arm in a sling, followed behind.

"So, it really *was* you, Jollux!" Big G said. "I never would've thought a small-timer like you could have pulled it off."

"But I told you," the other one protested.

"I know, Max," Big G replied. "I know."

"What did you do to my butler?" Jollux asked.

"You're going to need another one of those..." Big G replied with a sneer. He surveyed the broken glass and bent vegetation, the dome above riddled with bullet holes. "Well, well," he said. "I guess the shoe is on the other foot."

"I don't wear shoes."

"Never mind!" Big G shouted, waving the submachine gun. "Any last words, Jollux?"

Jollux steepled his long fingers.

"You're the owner of the largest casino in Ashetown," he said, "and I'm a loan shark owed millions by wealthy nobles for their gambling debts. I don't see why we couldn't combine our resources together."

"And sweep all this ugliness under the rug?" Big G replied, considering the proposal.

"Yes."

A devilish grin appeared on Big G's face.

"I don't think so," he said, pulling the trigger on the submachine gun. In a cloud of acrid smoke, Jollux rolled backwards off his bench, bullet holes in the center of his chest. He lay dead among his precious plants.

"Why'd you do that, boss?" Max asked.

"There can only be one big fish in *this* pond," Big G replied, pleased with his response.

Max stared blankly.

"Anyway…" Big G said with a sigh, "go tell the boys that the drinks are on me tonight!"

"You got it, boss," Max replied.

"But just the first *two* drinks," Big G said. "Let's not go crazy..."

At the end of the day, the business district of Regalis began to wind down as the shadows of skyscrapers stretched across the busy streets. Office workers poured out of the buildings, eager to get home, even if their home was nothing more than a wildly overpriced studio apartment.

Martel sat on a park bench, ignoring the pigeons while counting the worker drones shuffling by. A woman with red hair, wearing a lab coat, stopped and sat down beside him. Martel didn't like the smug grin on her face.

"I guess you think I should thank you?" the detective asked.

"It seems appropriate under the circumstances," Doctor Sprouse replied. "Did you read my little note?"

Martel pulled a folded piece of paper out of his pocket.

"For Martel," he read, "from a friend."

"I thought the *friend* part was a nice touch..."

"Cute," he remarked.

Sprouse turned her critical eyes on him. "Come now, Thomas, I saved your life!"

"I should've stayed in a coma," he replied. "I could've used the sleep."

The doctor crossed her arms with a grunt.

"It seems funny how quickly you came up with an antidote," Martel continued. "Almost like you were working on it beforehand."

"Well, you brought me a sample, didn't you?" she replied.

"No, I mean *before* that."

Sprouse gazed around at the people passing by. "You're not wearing a wire, are you?"

"Not at the moment," Martel said.

"It doesn't matter anyway," she went on. "Warlock Industries is untouchable even if you were."

"Warlock was responsible for Lotus all along, wasn't it?" Martel asked.

"For a long time, I've had an idea for weaponizing chem addiction," she replied. "The hard part was getting a big enough sample size to see if it's effective."

"So, you decided to use the general population as your guinea pigs?"

"Something like that."

"You're a monster," Martel said.

"Don't be crass," Sprouse replied. "It's all in the name of science..."

"And to make sure Lotus spread as effectively as possible, you hired Jollux to do your dirty work."

"We didn't so much *hire* him as help facilitate his rise in the community."

"Those mercs that were acting as his muscle..." Martel started.

"Warlock paramilitary forces," Sprouse said. "It was also an opportunity for them to learn asymmetrical, urban warfare tactics. I'm sure the training will come in handy down the road..."

"You gave Jollux the chems and the forces to make sure he'd spread Lotus far and wide," Martel said. "But then you withdrew both. Why?"

"The experiment was over," Sprouse said with a casual shrug. "Jollux was no longer needed."

"That's cold."

The doctor stood up and began to leave.

"And then there's the antidote," Martel continued.

Sprouse stopped and sat back down again. "Yes?"

"The government bought millions of doses," the detective said.

"Yes?" Sprouse asked again.

"Sounds lucrative."

Sprouse rolled her eyes. "You really *are* a detective, aren't you!"

"It just seems to me that the antidote is where the money is, not the original chems."

"If you must know," Sprouse said, "the Warlock board wasn't entirely sold on the idea of weaponizing Lotus, so I suggested we also sell the cure."

"And they agreed to that?"

"They ate it up!" Sprouse said with a hint of pride. "They even gave me a new *lab*."

Now it was Martel's turn to stand.

"What do you intend to do with this information?" the doctor asked him.

"What *can* I do?" he replied. "Like you said, Warlock Industries is untouchable."

"You could shoot me?" she suggested, practically daring him. "Get revenge for all those I've hurt?"

Martel reached into his coat, his fingers touching the cold metal of Maxwell.

"I could," Martel said, removing his hand and letting it fall to his side. "But I won't."

"Why?" Sprouse asked, genuinely curious.

"Because it wouldn't make a damn bit of difference," Martel replied and walked away into the darkening twilight.

Outside the Regalis city limits, Lefty Lucy and her adopted son, Roland, sat at a low table in the middle of a floor covered by tatami mats. From a porcelain teapot, Lucy poured tea into three small cups, offering one of the cups to a woman also sitting at the table. Lady Veber took the tea while attempting to stuff the rest of her dress under the table, producing a billowing canopy of light blue taffeta.

"Thank you," Lady Veber said.

Her face revealing nothing, Lucy handed a cup to Roland, though most of the public knew him better as *Jack Groen*.

"It's good to be back home," he admitted. "It feels like I've been sleepwalking lately…"

Lady Veber patted him on the leg. "Don't worry, Jack. I'll take good care of you." Seeing a muscle around Lucy's eye twitching, Lady Veber commented on the decor, "This is such a lovely home. Sparse, but *functional.*"

Lucy raised her cup, but her eyes remained locked on Lady Veber who laughed uncomfortably.

"As the Imperial Regent," Lady Veber went on, "I want to assure you that I will do everything in my power to protect your son. The palace can be a treacherous place at times, but it's where he belongs."

"Well," Jack said, "it's been a lot to get used to. I'm still not sure this was a good idea…"

Lady Veber gave him a reassuring smile.

"You're from one of the Five Families, Jack," she said. "It's your birthright."

"But you could have at least *asked* me before you nominated me for emperor," he replied, to which Lucy nearly dropped her cup.

"You didn't know?" Jack asked her.

His foster mother cleared her throat but said nothing.

"I should probably apologize," Lady Veber said, "to *both* of you, but it's important, Jack, that you realize what a tremendous opportunity this is. The thought of Tagus or even Prince Richard becoming emperor was more than I could bear."

Lucy glared.

"I think my mother is saying it wasn't your decision to make," Jack said.

"Perhaps," Lady Veber replied, "but someone had to. The Imperium teetered between the iron fist of Rupert Tagus and the dynastic ambitions of Richard Augustus. I did what I thought was right…"

They sat in awkward silence until Jack spoke.

"It's pretty incredible if you think about it," he said with a grin. "I'm going to be emperor!"

Lady Veber laughed. "Yes, you are!"

Lucy's expression softened and she poured more tea into Lady Veber's cup.

"And with any luck," Lady Veber said after taking a sip, "you won't get assassinated!"

Jack coughed a little of his tea back into the cup.

"Wait, what?" he asked.

For the continuing saga of the Imperium Chronicles,
watch for the next volume in the series,
The Elves of Andromeda.

CHARACTER LIST

Augustus, Emperor Hector: Patriarch of the Augustus family and current emperor of the Imperium.

Augustus, Lady Lilith: Wife of Prince Richard Augustus.

Augustus, Mason: Baby son of Prince Richard and Lady Lilith Augustus.

Augustus, Prince Alexander: Son of the Emperor and black sheep of the Augustus family.

Augustus, Prince Richard: First son of Emperor Augustus.

Benson: Butlerbot of Lord Devlin Maycare. Replaced the previous robot, Bentley, after he was destroyed.

Black, Magnus: A mysterious hitman with ties to both Imperial Intelligence and criminal syndicates.

Burke, Harold: Former attaché to Lord Tagus III. Deceased.

Burkebot ("Burke"): An execubot employed by Lord Tagus III. Named after Tagus' former attaché, Harold Burke.

Crawley, Detective: An unscrupulous detective of the Regalis Police Department. Former partner of Thomas Martel.

Davenport, Eugene ("Ducky"): College friend of Lord Winsor Woodwick and Lord Radford Groen.

Demona, Ta: A ruthless agent for the Psi Lords who uses her abilities to collect information.

Dingus, Homicide Detective: Martel's name for a detective on the Regalis P.D.

Dolores: A computer program serving as Thomas Martel's secretary. Strong Long Island accent.

Doric, Jessica: Head of research for the Maycare Institute of Xeno Studies.

Flax, Sylvia: Famous news anchor for VOX News.

G, Big: Tikarin leader of the Si-Sawat crime syndicate and proprietor of the Fat Cat Casino.

Grayson, Lord: A sports rival of Lord Maycare.

Groen, Jack: Son of Lord Robert and Lady Josephine Groen.

Groen, Lady Josephine: Wife of Lord Robert Groen, killed along with her husband.

Groen, Lord Radford: An aristocrat often found gambling with life-long friend, Lord Woodwick.

Groen, Lord Robert: An important member of the Groen family, killed along with his wife.

Groen, Lord Vincent: Representative of the Groen family at the Imperial Conclave.

Hogug, Mayor: The Gordian mayor of Kurkslag and the boss of a criminal syndicate.

Ivanovich, Gregor: Boss of the Cyberpunks gang.

Jollux ("Gelatinous Bob"): Loan shark and chem lord.

Lucy, Lefty: Bodyguard to Prince Alexander and former member of the Red Lotus syndicate. Foster mother to Roland.

Martel, Detective Thomas: Private detective and former police detective in the Regalis PD. Former partner with Detective Crawley.

Maycare, Lord Devlin: Famous sportsman and playboy. Founder of the Maycare Institute of Xeno Studies.

Max: Tikarin enforcer for the Si-Sawat syndicate, and Big G's right-hand man.

Montros, Lady Olivia: Representative of the Montros family at the Imperial Conclave.

Munge, Mister: Criminal enforcer for Kid Vicious.

O'Shea, Shady: Criminal contact of Thomas Martel.

Pitt: A mysterious man who first brought Roland to Lefty Lucy.

Red: Gordian bartender of the Sous-Sol.

Riff, Henry: Overly excitable assistant to Jessica Doric.

Rion, Louis: Cerulean owner of the Sous-Sol. Francophile.

Sprouse, Doctor: Geneticist working for Warlock Industries.

Roland: A teenager raised by Lefty Lucy.

Solan, Kanet: High-ranking member of the Psi Lords.

Tagus II, Lord Rupert: Former patriarch of the Tagus family and father of Lord Tagus III. Deceased.

Tagus III, Lord Rupert: Recently pardoned exile and now patriarch of the Tagus family.

Veber, Lady Rebecca: Matriarch of the Veber family.

Veber, Philip: Lady Veber's son. Deceased.

Vicious, Kid: Boss of the Griefer gang.

Ward: Gregor Ivanovich's bodyguard.

Wingus, Homicide Detective: Martel's name for a detective on the Regalis P.D.

Woodwick, Lady Candice ("Candy"): Niece of Lord Winsor Woodwick, and girlfriend of Lord Devlin Maycare.

Woodwick, Lord Winsor ("Winnie"): A noble of English descent and friend of Lord Radford Groen and Lord Devlin Maycare. Uncle of Lady Candice Woodwick.

GLOSSARY

Acaz: Lord Devlin Maycare's starship.

Aldorus: The home planet of the Imperial government.

Ashetown: A district of Regalis where the poorest of the city live.

Augmentor Sisterhood: A monastic sisterhood who worship technology, slowly adding cybernetic implants until they ascend to full robotic conversion. Found on the planet Technas Delphi.

Augustus: One of the Five Families, represented by a two-headed eagle.

Blood Ball: A violent sport similar to rugby played by non-humans.

Boneyards: An area of Ashetown where discarded machines and robots are dumped.

Boneyard Bruisers: A popular Blood Ball team.

braZos: The largest consumer mega-corporation in the Imperium, offering every product imaginable from its nodesphere site. Their boxes display a large letter Z on the side.

braZbots: Delivery robots for the braZos mega-corporation.

Cerulean: A race of blue-skinned mimics known for appropriating the characteristics of other races.

Chems: Street jargon for drugs.

Conclave, Imperial: A meeting of the Five Families to decide the next emperor.

Credit stick: A small storage device loaded with electronic currency.

Cyberpunks: An Ashetown street gang led by Gregor Ivanovich.

Dahl: An ancient race dedicated to the accumulation of knowledge. Physically slight, they coincidentally resemble elves of human folklore. Several sub-species of Dahl exist in Andromeda.

Dark Psi: A school of psionics, outlawed by the Dahl, that can transform flesh and reanimate dead tissue.

Draconians: A fierce, reptilian race.

Dûrndûran: A Gordian word meaning both "hello" and "go have sex with yourself."

Embassy Row: Area of the West End where foreign consulates are located.

Emissary Hotel: Exclusive hotel located near the Embassy Row area of Regalis. Home of the Grove restaurant.

Eudora Prime: A planet on the border of the Imperium where the Kamal Maut can be found.

Fat Cat Casino: A large gambling house on Regalis run by Big G.

Five Families: The most powerful houses of the Imperial nobility. Direct descendants of the captains from the surviving sleeper ships.

Fogmore Gardens: Cemetery where the Imperial family is buried. Located adjacent to the Palace grounds.

Galanis: A planet largely owned and controlled by the Groen family.

Gordian: A race of stubborn, boar-like humanoids with pig noses and tusks. Physically stocky, but shorter than the average human.

Grarfell ("Gray Old Man"): Home world of the Gordian race.

Greenwood Country Club: Exclusive golfing club for the rich and famous located in the West End of Regalis.

Griefers: An Ashetown street gang led by Kid Vicious.

Groen: One of the Five Families, represented by a botonée cross.

Grove, The: Restaurant located inside the Emissary Hotel. Famous for its brunch.

Hypersled: A type of rocket-powered snow sled used for racing.

Imperium: An empire largely controlled by humans. Founded 700 years ago, after humans arrived in sleeper ships from Earth after an 800-year journey.

Kamal Maut ("Death Lotus"): A terrifying creature evolved from fungi that can exhale a cloud of poisonous spores.

Kurkslag: A Gordian city-state located beneath the surface of Grarfell.

Lotus: A new chem that users ingest by letting a petal-like tab dissolve on their tongue. Causes users to fall into a deep sleep and have vivid dreams. Highly addictive.

Lotus Eaters: Name for those who use Lotus.

Lokeren: A water planet featuring tropical archipelagos and the home of the Veber family estate.

LSV: Name for a commonly used chem.

Mad Hatter: Name for a commonly used chem.

Max Jō: A brand of extreme coffee.

Maxwell: Detective Martel's handgun, a brushed chrome-plated, .44 Magnum with a thick, heavy barrel.

Maycare Institute of Xeno Studies: An organization founded by Lord Devlin Maycare and run by Professor Jessica Doric. The purpose of the institute is to find and take possession of xeno technology before it falls into the hands of disreputable parties such as Warlock Industries.

Middleton: A district of Regalis inhabited by large businesses and, in general, middle-class neighborhoods.

Montros: One of the Five Families, represented by a rose.

Mudderfield Downs: Name of a horse track in the city of Regalis.

Nobles ("Aristocracy"): Families of the Imperium who are directly descended from the crews of the sleeper ships. The most powerful of these are called the Five Families.

Nodesphere: A vast network of computers (i.e., an internet).

Polar Run: Name of a hypersled track located at the south pole of the planet Aldorus.

Psi Lords: A secretive data cartel that uses dark psi and espionage to gather and sell information to the highest bidder.

Psionics: Special mental abilities common among Dahl and related sub-species.

Regalis: Capital city and seat of government of the Imperium, located on the planet Aldorus.

Regalis Police Department ("Regalis PD"): The collection of precincts that make up the Regalis police.

Regency Heights Sanatorium: A mental health facility consisting of over thirty acres of wooded, gently sloping land outside of Regalis.

Rey Sol ("Sun King"): Name of Devlin Maycare's maritime yacht.

Saint Eligius Royal Hospital: A hospital catering exclusively to the rich and powerful of Imperial society, including the Emperor's own family.

Si-Sawat: A crime syndicate made up of Tikarin and led by Big G.

Sous-Sol, Le ("The Basement"): A bar owned by Louis Rion, located in Ashetown at the corner of Marlowe and Vine.

Starling: Starship owned by Magnus Black.

Tagus: One of the Five Families, represented by a lion.

Technas Delphi: Ta Demona's home world, run by a female-centered theocracy called the Augmentors.

TeeHee Tea: A popular brand of tea, believed to contain mood-altering ingredients.

Tikarin: A feline race slightly smaller than an average human.

Transmat: A transportation device that dematerializes travelers in one location and then beams them to a new location where they are rematerialized.

Tubby Wubby: Genetically engineered teddy bear "toys" that became psychotic once they were sold to the public.

Veber: One of the Five Families, represented by a scallop shell.

VOX News: A news organization with a near-monopoly share of the broadcast market throughout the Imperium.

Warlock Industries: A mega-corporation operating throughout the Imperium, specializing in military hardware, advanced technology, and genetic experimentation.

West End: The richest district of Regalis. Also, the location of most Imperial government buildings.

Xeno: A non-human.

Zahmetli Hamami: A Turkish bath visited by Lord Devlin Maycare and Lord Eugene "Ducky" Davenport.

ABOUT THE AUTHOR

W. (William) H. Mitchell was born in Omaha, NE and graduated from the University of Nebraska-Lincoln with a degree in English. He lives with his wife and cats outside of Kansas City.

Follow him on his website at WHMitchellFiction.com